Talk

KATHE KOJA

SQUARE FISH

Farrar, Straus and Giroux

SQUARE
FISH

An Imprint of Macmillan

Library of Congress Cataloging-in-Publication Data
Koja, Kathe.
    Talk / Kathe Koja.— 1st ed.
        p.   cm.
    Summary: Hoping to escape from himself for a while, Kit auditions for
a controversial school play and discovers his talent for acting, struggles
with coming out, and both he and his costar face crises in their view of
themselves and in their close relationships. Told from two points of view.
    [1. Coming out (Sexual orientation)—Fiction.   2. Homosexuality—
Fiction.   3. Theater—Fiction.   4. Self-perception—Fiction.   5. Schools—
Fiction.]   I. Title.

PZ7.K8312Tal 2005
[Fic]—dc22
                                                        2003069366

        ISBN-13: 978-0-312-37605-5 / ISBN-10: 0-312-37605-7

        Originally published in the United States
            by Farrar, Straus and Giroux
        First Square Fish Edition: February 2008
        Square Fish logo designed by Filomena Tuosto
            Designed by Nancy Goldenberg
            10   9   8   7   6   5   4   3   2   1
                www.squarefishbooks.com

To Rick and Aaron, as always,
and to Allan from Arkansas,
with respect and affection

My thanks:
to Rob Derminer, for access
to Helene Dworkin, for the interview
to Kimberly Grover and the wonderful
Affirmations Youth Group
to Stephanie Nichols and the talented
Berkley High School cast and crew
and to Lia Wolock, for very dramatic examples.

Special thanks to Rick Lieder, Aaron Mustamaa,
Chris Schelling, and Frances Foster.

Talk

1

So there I am, too-bright theater light and "What is this?" I say to Carma, flipping through the blue script booklet full of broken lines, it doesn't make any sense. "Is this supposed to be like poetry, or what? '. . . finish what you started. REED: It starts with me. It ends with you.' Why is it written like—"

"Because," with exaggerated patience, pushing back her mop of hair, even moppier than mine, "you are a dupe. . . . Look, they give you your line and most of the line right before yours, get it? So you don't have to put the whole play in each script."

"But how am I supposed to know where I am?"

"Because instead of checking out all the cute guys in crew, you've actually been paying attention to—"

"Leads down front, please."

Her sharp elbow digging into my side: "That's you. Go."

"Go where?"

"Where they are," with another dig to send me down the slope of red carpet, red-and-black diamonds, endless pattern like infinity, why am I noticing this? and not the teacher, no, the director, no, Mick, *Call me Mick* with his arms crossed, head back, eyes half closed but you know he's watching. *Leads down front* which means me and Lindsay Walsh, who's standing arms-crossed next to Mick like she's a director, too. When I walk up her gaze goes straight through me, as if there's not enough of me to make it stick, but he looks right in my face: "Kit," sharp, no, *crisp*, like a finger snap. His eyes are pale gray, like water over stones. "I need you where she is. I need you two to be together. Right?"

"Uh, right." How would I know? I lean against the stage, a step beside Lindsay who keeps ignoring me; Mick stands in front of us both, swivels on his heels and "Here they are," he says, "here it is. *Talk*," to the people scattered in the seats, the rest of the cast, does he mean he wants them to— oh I get it, he's saying we're the play, Lindsay and me. Is that what he's saying? But then what about them?

I don't understand any of this. But that's OK, that's why I'm here. I wanted to go someplace where I could be someone else, where I could—lose myself. Just for a little while. So when Carma dared me—she never thought I would, I know, which is partially why I did—I went with her to auditions, and read for Reed, that's my part. Reed the lead. And I got it.

Mick rubs his chin, the blond glint of on-purpose stubble. He's wearing all black, black jeans, black sneakers, black collarless shirt. "What these two are going to create," he says, "is surface tension. A whole world in a bubble. Right? And we're all going to ride along in that bubble."

The people in the seats nod, or tilt their heads; a couple of them I know to say hi to, Carma's thespian friends, she always says it like that: *my thespian friends*. Because Carma's in crew, and they're actors, and the two don't usually mix. I guess in some schools everybody does everything, like in one show you're Juliet and the next you're painting scenery. But not here at Faulkner. *It's apartheid,* Carma says. *And we like it that way.*

"We don't have a lot of time, people: just ten weeks. And *Talk* is a demanding production. To say the least. There are adult groups I've worked with I wouldn't dream of using for this kind of stuff. But I believe you can do it."

"Like *A Doll's House,*" Lindsay says. "Everyone thought that would be hard. But it wasn't." She sounds bored, as if she shouldn't have to sit through the pep talk like the rest of us. Lindsay is president of the Drama Club, queen of the senior girls, Lola, the other lead. *Lola, a Resistance fighter.* That's all it says on the cast sheet. Like mine says *Reed, interrogator.*

Mick rubs his chin again. "Read-through tomorrow, cast *and* crew, everybody, I want you there. Right? Three-fifteen, in the Jewel," which means the Jewel Box Theater, not the auditorium, everyone groans, Carma bitches all the way out to the parking lot: "—need crew there, we're not thespians, are we? Plus it's always so hot in there, you put like three people onstage and it turns into a total sweat lodge. Thank god we don't do the plays there." She cranks her car furiously, it catches, dies, catches again. Worry-bead rosaries dangle pink-and-gold from the rearview mirror, soft crackle underfoot from a dozen old Bib's Bagel bags and "Well?" as she zooms out into traffic, the last dregs of after-school gridlock. "So what do you think, Reed? You glad you did it?"

I put on my blue sunglasses, deep aquarium blue, the undersea world of Kit Webster and "I don't know," I say. "I didn't do it yet."

Then she wants me to go with her, to Bib's of course, *Oh come on I'm starving* but even though I love Carma, she's been like my best friend forever, I just need to be alone sometimes, in my room, lair, whatever. . . . My mom gave up trying to clean it long ago, so she just leaves the door shut, leaves my laundry folded in a basket outside the door, a peeling wicker basket our cat is slowly destroying—that and the window-seat cushion, unraveling green brocade, Pixy's other scratching post. The window seat is why I picked this room for mine, way back when we first moved here. It was like a, a crow's nest or something, tree-top high, I used to take my comic books and a can of Coke and sit there for hours, the sun on my face, then my hands, then my feet, then gone. Outside I could hear kids, boys, playing ball, skateboarding, being with each other. I'd open the window as wide as I could, so I could hear them better.

I can't fit like that in the window seat anymore, so now

it's turned into Pixy's spot, big fat yellow cat who barely glances up when I walk in, toss my stuff down, turn on the computer to check my mail. Nothing much: a couple of jokes from Carma, a how-are-you from my Uncle Sean. I lean back on the bed with the blue script book and the handout from Mick—cast list, the tentative schedule—but before I start reading I reach up, like I always do, to touch his smiling face: last year's Student Art Fest, Carma took the picture, I made a blow-up print at Kinko's. Red shirt, dark eyes, big sunny grin like all the world's a party: Pablo Roy, jazz band, Forensics and fencing team, last year's first gay Harvest King. Pablo, my true and secret love.

TIME *An indeterminate modern year. It could be the future; it could be today.*

SETTING *A claustrophobic interior; a holding cell; four square walls with no way out. There is a door with a crash bar, and one barred window showing neither dark nor light, only constant gray. A small metal table, one chair, and a three-legged stool.*

A WORD ABOUT THE CHARACTERS *Talk can utilize as many as twenty or as few as five actors: the core cast of Reed, Lola, the Doctor, the Judge, and the Boy. The roles of Runners and Reporters are expandable to accommodate larger ensembles if desired.*

REED (*entering with clipboard, pen, and bulky gray bulletproof vest*) Good morning, Lola. Were you able to get some rest?

. . . matter to a bully.

REED What matters to us both, I think, is the truth. You know it. I need it. (*Sits.*) Please don't make this into something it's not.

. . . with the Resistance. You can't prove—

REED (*kindly*) The law moves on suspicion, not proof. It has to, for safety's sake. So in the interest of safety—

your safety, too—that law puts you here, until you and I can establish a basis for dialogue. (*Smiles.*) It's a matter of trust, really.

. . . all you want, forever. But I won't tell you anything.

REED Interrogate? Oh no, no, not at all. You and I are just going to talk.

2

———◆———

"Kit who?"

"I told you, I don't know." My coffee tastes like sludge, just completely bitter; I take Ashley's peach tea instead. The Quad is so noisy, it's ridiculous we're even here. "Some kid. He's not in Drama or anything." Frankly I'd expected to be, you know, consulted at least, I mean I am the president of Drama, plus the lead, Mick cast me first of anyone. So for him to just spring this kid on me, I don't even know if he can act or—

"What part did you get, Ashley?" Liz sucks at her SuperShake. Why does she drink those things? They're nothing but liquid fat and she's already like five pounds overweight.

Ashley frowns. "I didn't try out." Liz and I both look at each other, Liz rolls her eyes. We both know that the reason Ashley didn't try out is she wanted Lola and I was already Lola, I mean as soon as I read it I knew.

This is my last play, except for the musical which is in the spring and I probably won't have time and anyway I don't like musicals that much. I mean, I can sing fine, but— So I wanted something special, something that was going to look really good on my resumé. My parents—my *mother*, God—wanted me to go early-decision to Juilliard. But I don't know. . . . Maybe Yale? Or a conservatory? Reeny Kemp's at Juilliard. I understudied Reeny Kemp freshman year, in *Anne Frank*.

Across the Quad, past the rows of planters and the freaks handing out their freaky little pamphlets, I can see Blake, hanging all over some little slut of a sophomore and checking to make sure I'm watching, like this is supposed to shatter my heart to pieces or something. Well, I've got some news for Blake, which I might deliver today at read-through. He's one of the Runners, even though I told Mick he was too dim to learn a lot of lines but *We need someone big for the crash-bar scene,* says Mick so OK, fine, Blake can carry heavy objects. But he's not what *I* need anymore. In a way it's not even Blake I'm sick of, it's just the, the sameness, all the Blake-types I've had since forever: they all wear Custa sneakers and they all drive two-seaters or Jeeps, they all play sports, they all can't wait to get my pants off and then afterwards have nothing to say. . . . At first I was going to wait till after the Harvest dance—other schools have Homecoming; we have Harvest—or maybe even our anniversary, but why? I don't want his stupid dozen roses and Cristal, I can buy my own champagne. And I don't know if I want to be Harvest Queen again. It was fun last year with Pablo, I mean for a homo he is really sweet, and a good dancer, god. And because he's gay it was like a big joke, everyone had fun. But this year Blake'll probably be King, so no way, not me. Let Ashley do it. She can have my sloppy seconds, she's used to it.

Now "Ready?" says Liz, sucking up the last of her shake, slurp-slurp. "I have to run to the store, I need to get some cigarettes—"

"Smoking gives you wrinkles, don't you know that? Plus your car smells like an ashtray." I finish Ashley's tea, slide off the bench. "If you really want to lose weight, why don't you just stop eating?"

Ashley laughs her high little mouse-laugh. Liz turns away, throws her empty cup in the trash, hard. Blake detaches himself from the sophomore slut, but by the time he gets halfway across the Quad, I'm gone.

3

—————◆—————

"Runner Four. Line."

"Um—wait, wait I got it—'Is this it, Doctor? Is this what you want?'"

"'Who.'"

"What?"

"'*Who* you want.' Line again."

I hear Carma's snicker, somewhere behind me. Crew sits apart, in a pocket of its own, aloof from the knot of thespians. I sit apart, in a pocket of my own, the envelope of apartness I've had, used, forever. It's like safety glass: it keeps people from being able to hurt you, mostly, and you can still see everything that happens.

Like Blake Tudor, now, sweating as he gives the line again, thick jock finger underlining his way through the script: "'Is this it, Doctor? Is this who you want?' Right?"

"Just the line."

"'Is this—'" as Dan Castle, the Doctor, overlaps him: "'Bring the boy into the lab. Now.'"

"'No!'" Lindsay Walsh's voice rings out, desperate, passionate; she gives me chills, the way she reads. I know what people say about her, Carma, the other girls, I know she's the bitch of the school, the bitch of the world but man, can she act. She makes everybody else look like, well, like high school kids. She makes me want to be as good as she is, or at least try, try as hard as I can. "'He's just a child, he doesn't know—Reed, stop this, you can stop this, even you must see this is wrong!'"

"'He refuses to talk to us, Lola. It's out of my hands.'" I try to make my voice calm, regretful, even genuinely sorry; with lava, pure red lava seething underneath. This Reed guy is evil, I think, but still human, he can still be reached. Lola is reaching him, despite everything, Lola is cutting down to the bone. . . . Actually this is a really cool play. If only everybody in it was as good as Lindsay. "'I intend no harm, I never have, to him, to—you, never. *Never*. I only want you to tell the truth. You can save him, save us both, Lola, it's up to you.'"

Silence, Lindsay hisses a sigh, like steam through a crack.

"Runner Four," Mick's whipcrack voice, "*line*."

"Um. 'Is this—' No, wait. 'Come on.'"

"Runner Four—" looking at his notes, "Blake, why aren't you following along? I shouldn't have to keep prompting you."

"Sorry."

Blake scowls, not at Mick but at Lindsay. Where she's sitting the light hits her just right, makes her blond hair a glimmering halo, casts a shadow fetchingly across her face, maybe she sat there on purpose—well yeah, of course she did—but it works. She looks like an angel, some other-worldly medieval saint. . . . Although I'd rather look at Blake, even if he is a troglodyte. I was on the swim team with him, way back in middle school, before he bulked up, and before I figured out I'd better get off the swim team.

Lindsay makes another little sound. Mick sighs, rubs his chin. "Don't say sorry. Say your lines when it's time to say them."

Sullenly, "'Come on.'"

"Mick," Lindsay says in her own voice, that cool half-irritated drawl, "I need a break."

"OK. Fine, so do I," and he calls a break, ten minutes, instant chatter as half the room bolts for the john, the other half for the water table, Blake turns for Lindsay who turns away, another kind of play? as I feel Carma's hands clap down on my shoulders: "Hey, boy. Having fun yet?"

Sweat on my back, sticky and damp; she was right, it's amazingly hot in here. The blue-plush sixty-seat Jewel Box, gift to Faulkner from one of its million rich alumni, maybe someone who was hoping his kid would play Hamlet. Not that they ever do any Shakespeare, although at least Faulkner stays away from the obvious: *Kiss Me, Kate*, *The Music Man*, stuff that's been done a thousand times. Not like *Talk*. Which according to my mom is a surprising choice: *Gutsy*, she called it, when she saw the script on the table. My mom admires gutsy.

Now I lean back as Carma squeezes my shoulders, her famous two-minute massage; she's got big hands, and a grip like a wrestler's, from hefting all those power tools. "Fun," I say, "oh sure. More than poor Blake, anyway."

"Is he not a lummox? His brain wouldn't even make a good doorstop. Herr Direktor only cast him because—"

"—because he's Lindsay's honey," from over my other shoulder, Jefrey-with-one-F, another longtime crew dog. FAULKNER DRAMA T-shirt, his hair in a hundred small braids, like a two-inch forest above his face. He smiles at me, bright sideways smile; his front teeth are just a little crooked. "You sounded really good, Kit."

"No, Lindsay's the one who—"

A loud metal *screee!* from a folding chair shoved sideways, toppling hard across the tiny stage: everyone stops, stares as Blake storms down the aisle, and out, Lindsay shrugs and takes her seat again and "OK," Mick claps his hands, "break's over, let's go, people. —What happened to, what's his name? Blake?"

Everyone looks at Lindsay, who shrugs again; she's smiling, a one-sided, satisfied smile, like two and two really do make four. Or two minus one is one. "He's gone."

Carma rolls her eyes, gives my shoulders one last squeeze; Jef says something in her ear. Mick sighs again, a loud titanic gust. "Well, he can't be *gone* until I replace him. . . . OK, OK, whatever. All right, Lindsay, you can pick up from 'Come on'—"

—and she does, immediate, amazing, her voice ringing and rippling through what comes next, the long barbed-wire speech, *fear's the real barbed wire, fear's what holds us in, fences us from our desires, from what we know belongs to us* and it's as if she really is Lola the resistance fighter, grimy from prison, weak from her hunger strike but on fire with what she knows is true, what she loves, just listening makes you love it too, makes you want to rush out and scale a mountain or storm a building or give your life for some wonderful cause, sweeps you away like I'm swept away as I open my mouth, say my line but now I'm not Kit saying a line, I'm Reed answering her, Reed who all of a sudden like a lightning flash I see, I *get*: he's in love with Lola, in love with the freedom she represents but scared of it too, oh god so scared and that's why he says "save us *both*," in that line before, that's why he says—

"This world doesn't work the way you think it does, dream love faith worth nothing in the fire, *nothing*. They *burn* people like you, Lola, they cut you to pieces and call it the common good! The barbed wire's there for a reason, a good reason, it's— Because they can't bear what you represent! Because they're afraid!"

"Are you afraid? Reed, tell me. Are you afraid?"

Pause, it says, and I do, I have to, I can barely get a breath; my eyes are squeezed closed. Then "No," I say without the breath, without air, as if I'm caught in a vacuum, suffocating on the lie. "But you should be."

So soft it's barely there, her voice: "Of what?"

Like lead: "Of me."

Silence: and then applause, a bright battering sound that shocks my eyes open, my face turns instantly red. Carma's calling something but it's Lindsay I look at first, Lindsay smiling as people clap, a different smile than before and for just that one second our eyes meet; she sees me, now.

And Mick's crow, "Bravo! On a first run-through! Let's go on to the yard scene, OK?" and we do, everyone riding the wave now, Dan Castle the Doctor and the freshman who plays the Boy, the yard scene and the failed escape and the fire, and me and Lindsay, Reed and Lola at the end, on-stage we would be, will be face-to-face, mouth to mouth almost, breathing for each other—and then the last lines are said and it's over, firecracker hand-claps, people talking all at once and "Yeah boy!" Carma hugging me one-armed, Jef and the other crew kids around her, around me, all smiles and I smile back but it's like, what? coming to, coming down—disoriented, that's the word. Like the *Talk* world runs parallel to this one, and I don't know where I am yet, here or there; which is weird, very weird but exciting too, like the law of gravity's just been repealed, like anything can happen now—

"—Kit?" Mick beside me, eyes ashine, like he's half in that other world, too. "You've never acted before, seriously? In a youth group, or drama camp, or—?"

"No."

"Well. I must have known, I cast you, right? —Same time tomorrow, OK, all the principals," and off he goes, and we go, me and Carma to Bib's where she buys me a chocolate-raisin bagel and a mocha crème, *my treat*, feet on the seat and she can't stop talking about how amazing I was, see didn't she *tell* me, didn't she *know* that if I just auditioned I'd—but "Lindsay's the one," I say, peering at her over my sunglasses. "She's what got me going."

Hand through her hair, that springy hedge of brown; she sucks her straw, more noise than necessary, makes a face but "True," she says at last; Carma always tells the truth in the end. "She was amazing, too."

4

On the floor, the phone against my head and I'm thinking about the run-through, god, I thought Mick was going to wet himself. Although I have to say I was surprised by that kid, what's his name? Kit. I mean I was sailing along, you know, just all Lola, thinking about how easy it was and how it would play onstage, thinking of how my dad would be down front, getting it down—he always has, from when I was a little girl. I remember being like three years old or something, in this yellow spangled fairy-princess dress, dancing around on the deck saying *Daddy, watch me play show!* And he'd take tons of pictures . . . I have like a million little movies, from playing show, and from all the camps I went to, day camps and summer camps and Drama Weekends, every performance, everything I ever did. And my mother'd sit and watch them all after-wards, and make these remarks—she still does, she never gives up—like *A little late on your line there* or *They can't hear you unless you speak up*, blah blah blah, like she's the director or something. At first I was kind of . . . upset. But later I just learned to tune it all out.

You can tune out the director, too, a lot of the time, I mean I *know* what a good performance is by now, I don't have to be told. Like that Kit kid. I didn't expect him to be able to, you know, return my serves the way he did, but he was right there. . . . It's too bad he's so dupey-looking, with that floppy hair and those horrible department store T-shirts, maybe he gets them from his girlfriend in crew. She looks like a clown. Why does Drama attract so many losers? the misfits, the ones who don't fit in anywhere else in school, the ones who aren't good at anything else. Or the wallpaper people, like what's-her-name who's playing the Judge—Alice Metsig, right. She's been in like a hun-dred shows here and I can never remember her name. Tells you something, doesn't it.

But I think this show is going to be what I want it to be, I really do. Sometimes you get that feeling—like when I was Nora in *Doll's House*, or Pegeen in *Playboy* at camp—you just know. And even though all we did was read-through, and even though Blake did his best to make a scene right in the middle of it—make a scene, that's funny, he can't even act!—I just know. This is going to be what I wanted it to be. This is going to be my show.

"—attention?" Ashley's voice through the phone, too

loud, like she's yelling right in my head. "Did you even hear what I *said*?"

"Of course I heard." Listening to Ashley is like watching TV, you can do it while you're busy with something else and not miss anything important. I sit up straight again, to fluff the squashed-up pillow, looking at the armoire all tacked with pictures, Pegeen and Nora and Ophelia and Sally Brown, all of them me, stepping stones to where I want to be: everywhere, everyone knowing who I am. And no more Blakes, but someone who's right for me, real for me, there for me like a guy should be—

"So should I tell him, or not?"

Tell who what? so "Sure," I say. Ashley's always telling some guy something, usually whatever he wants to hear. "Tell him anything you want."

5

———◆———

"Kit? Dinner."

My mom's signature two-knuckle knock, *tap-tap*, dinnertime already? I must have dozed. Haven't done that in a while, falling asleep after school, I used to do it all the time in sophomore year. Come home and just—disappear. Crawl into sleep like an animal crawls into a burrow, pull up the covers, anything to stop thinking. But I'm awake, now.

"So where's Dad?" at the table, she's ladling sauce over the pasta, something steamy and spicy, dark purple basil, tomatoes in chunks. Pixy lies under my chair, I can just see the white tip of his tail. "Chicago, still?"

"No, he's home—not home-home, but back in the office. He'll be here in a bit." My dad's a lawyer, he does a lot of traveling. He says *pro bono* is really

Latin for *economy class*, but he's proud of what he does, and so is my mom. So am I, really. Even though no one at my school would understand, even Carma: *Your dad sues people? For nothing?*

*It's not for nothing, Carm. It's for the public good. Like right now he's suing this one company, they were dumping crap in the water right where these people—*but she'd stopped listening so I stopped talking, some things you can't explain anyway. Like Mick: *You've never acted before, seriously?* Only all my life. Seriously. Acting like I was straight.

I remember when I knew I was different; I always felt different, but when you're little, you know, you take things in stride, like *up is up* and *water is wet* and *I like boys,* so what? It wasn't until later that I started to see, to feel, that there was a difference, that something was different in me.

And then in fifth grade, Mrs. Carver's class, two girls were calling me gay, and Mrs. Carver got really mad at them, said it was an ugly word, a terrible word. And then I got the lightning flash, and I thought: Oh my god, when they say *gay* they mean to be like *I* am? to feel like I feel about other boys? Is *that* what the deal is?

An ugly word, a terrible word.

"How's the play coming?" My mother sips her wine, a gentle ruby glow, the same color as her sweater. "You had rehearsal today?"

"Yeah. —Pixy, no," his pink inquisitive nose, he doesn't even like pasta but he'll beg for it anyway. "It's called," what is it called again? blocking? "Like where they show you where to sit and stand and all that, like walking you through it," although there isn't that much to show, most of it is just common sense: I'm in the authority position, so I'm behind the table. I want to intimidate Lola, so she's on the wobbly stool. Actually she moves around a lot more than I do: to the window, the door, leaning on the table to yell in my face—Lindsay can sure look ugly when she wants to, she can really—

"Well, I can't wait to see the show," my mom says. "I have to admit, I've never thought of Faulkner as a particularly progressive school, in fact if it wasn't for your father I'd've pulled you out of there long ago—" This is an old song, I can tune this verse out: Mom wants son in school where people are nice and not money-obsessed sex addicts, Dad says son has to learn how to live in the world we have, not the world we want. "—bound to be some flack, though, even from a school board as out of touch as Angie Tudor and her cronies—"

"What do you mean, flack? Pixy, down."

"Well, it's quite a controversial play, especially for a high school to put on. Those interrogation scenes are pretty brutal, don't you think? And that little boy is killed?"

"What little—oh right," the Boy, Nick Pantaleo; he gets tortured and dies. "I guess it is kind of brutal. "But movies and stuff are just as bad, right? and people see those all the time. And in Lit we're doing *A Clockwork Orange*, and that's *incredibly*—"

"It's not just that. These are their kids," she says, spooning Parmesan. "More cheese? No? —*Their kids* up on that stage, for everyone to watch. And the idea behind the play, that the self is revealed no matter what—*that's* threatening. Because what people want is for other people to think that they're good, to *believe* that they're good and not the way they really are: greedy, angry, and scared. Scared most of all."

Are you afraid? Reed, tell me.

Two Teenagers in Twenty, Coming Out Proud, "A High School Student Speaks Out about Homophobia." You bet I'm afraid. Not so much of the stuff they say—*faggot, fairy, cocksucker*, all the sticks and stones—but what they mean when they say it. *An ugly word, a terrible word.* Not that those girls were calling me a name, but what the name *meant*: that to be gay, to be what I was, was ugly and terrible. Who wouldn't be scared of that?

And sometimes—not at Faulkner much, but other schools for sure, and out in the world too—they do a lot more, a lot worse than call you names. Like what they did to Matthew Shepard. Or Harvey Milk. Or—

"—OK? Kit?"

"What?"

Fork poised, her gaze on me is loving, worried; I'm almost positive she knows, my dad too but it's not the kind of thing I'm going to just jump up and say: *Hey Mom, Dad, I'm gay, what's for dessert?* If they ever asked I'd tell them. Probably. But if they knew—my mother, especially, she'd be out the next morning buying a rainbow decal and going to PFLAG meetings and wearing STRAIGHT BUT NOT NAR-

ROW T-shirts and I don't think I'm ready for that much exposure just yet. So when she says "Are you OK?" with that extra little emphasis, eyebrows up and mouth down, her code for *I know something's not right and I want to help,* "I'm fine," I say, which is my code for *I know you want to help but you can't and anyway let's don't talk about it.* "Just thinking. . . . Mick said it was a difficult play, but I thought," it sounds silly now, "that he meant the lines or something."

"Well that too, I'm sure. It's all about the lines, the words, isn't it?" as the phone goes, the machine picks up but when I hear her voice— "—there, boy, so stop hiding—" "It's Carma," I say and "Ask her if she's had dinner yet," my mom calls. She loves Carma, she always did, ever since I first brought her home back in seventh grade, when she was still Carmen Jaworsky and I was still ghosting around friendless. Together we changed all that, made her into Carma and opened my closet door just the tiniest crack. So I could breathe. When I told her I was gay . . . I was so scared, I didn't really think she'd recoil in disgust and march off, I mean this was Carma, my friend, my best friend, my only friend, but still, I could barely get the words out. I just stood there, twisting and squeezing a piece of paper, some dumb handout from school. And she looked at me from under her bangs and said *Whoa, breaking news. I knew it before you did. Next topic, please.*

Now "The *movie,*" she says, as if we're already in the middle of a conversation and I should know exactly what she's talking about. She always does that; it's a pain in the ass. "Me, you. Ten minutes. Be on the stoop, boy, with your popcorn money."

"What movie? I'm eating dinner right now, I—"

"What movie, he says. The movie Pablo Roy is going to see, that's what movie. *Say You Will*, at the mall, nine minutes now, I'll pick you up."

LOLA (*leaning back; stiffly, she is in a certain amount of pain*) You wrap yourself in all those layers, like bandages on a wound: cop, interrogator, official of the government. Guardian of the public safety. But who are *you*, Reed, really? Or who were you, before you came here, scuttled into this place like a cockroach afraid of the kitchen light?

. . . think of bureaucrats. But there's no need to call names.

LOLA But names are what we are, aren't they? "Terrorist," that's your name for me, that's why you can stick me in this hole and torment me, because by calling me that name what you're really saying is that I'm no one worthy, I'm bad, in fact I'm even worse than bad: I'm *wrong*. And it's all right to hurt someone who's wrong, because she's barely even a person anymore, just a problem you're trying to correct. And if the problem doesn't come out right, you just erase it from the board. And feel nothing. Right?

But if the problem is a *person*, a real live sweating breathing person, with fears and desires, maybe desires like yours and maybe not, that's true, but once you know she's real, *I'm* real, then what do you do? Erase me if you don't like my answer? What you're doing is killing people, Reed, be very clear about that. First you give them a name that makes them easy to kill, and then you lock them up, and then—

. . . bring you here to debate.

LOLA Then what did you bring me here for? I thought you said you wanted to talk. (*Silence.*)
Would you like to know (*leaning over the table, face very close to* REED's) my name for you?

. . . matter.

LOLA But it does. So when you're ready, ask.
And I'll tell you.

6

"OK, OK," Mick clapping his hands like a ringmaster, like in the circus, trying to get the tiger to jump through the hoop. Sometimes he's such a stereotype, you know? in his black sneakers and theater T-shirts, today it's a Stratford shirt, like this is impressive or something. Big deal. Anybody can buy a souvenir. "Again, from 'stand for it,' Doctor. And this time don't just say it, *play* it."

Dan Castle rubs at his chin; he's growing a beard to make himself look older. It's completely not working, but Jenna—she's makeup—she can do miracles. I've already told her what I want Lola to look like: a little bruised, my hair tangled: but sexy. Like, you know, a hero. "The board won't stand for it, Reed. Or the Judge. There are protocols, you know. There are—"

"Who's doing my job?" Kit says. He sounds incredibly vicious, just the way Reed should sound. "Them or me? *You* or me? Are you angling to change careers, Doctor? Do you want to do what I do?" as he gets right up in Dan's face. Kit's not really big, just tall and skinny, but all of a sudden he's—enormous, he takes up all the room on the stage and I think, This is how people must feel when they watch me. Because when he's up there, when he's *on*, he's all you want to look at. . . . Where has he been *hiding*? God, could I have used him in *Doll's House*.

But then Mick, the asshole, jumps in and stops them, to make some dumb speech about subtext or something, how the AP Lit teachers are all worked up, they want to make sure we're getting it right, *he* wants to make sure because there's a lot of interest in this production, everyone's watching him to see how he brings off something that's so very blah blah blah. . . . He's always doing stuff like this, like he wants to draw attention to himself or something, he wants to be the star.

So I give a big loud sigh, to let him know nobody cares—

—and Kit looks up, out into the seats, like my sigh was his cue and "I know what I'm doing," he says, hard and rude, he's glaring down at Mick who sucks in his breath— but he's not Kit saying it, he's Reed, and Mick laughs, I laugh, Kit is Kit again and smiles and "OK," Mick says, grinning, "back to work. Reporters, you're up."

The Reporters file onstage, Kit and Castle get off, Kit hustling up the aisle till I snag his sleeve, make him stop and "You shut Mick up," I say. "Congratulations."

"Shucks," which is supposed to mean what? but he's smiling when he says it, that dupey shy cute smile, if he had a decent haircut he'd be almost, you know, hot and "How come," I ask, because I really want to know, "you've never been in any of the plays before? You're only like a hundred times better than anybody here, you blow them off the stage—what?" as he makes a face. "It's true, you're—"

"Don't," he says, very very quiet. "Lola, don't."

Lola? "I'm not Lola, I'm Lindsay," I say, and smile, but he's not joking; is he? I don't know, I can't tell but "You're both," he says; and what's *that* supposed to mean? "Be Lola for me, OK?" and gently tugs his sleeve away, heads back up the aisle to sit with who? oh his dumb crew girl-friend, how can *she* be *his* girlfriend? She looks like a bag of rags.

Be Lola for me.

What does that mean?

7

Carma squints, frowns, backspaces. Her desk is so covered with junk you can barely see her computer: sticky notes and soda cans, broken necklaces, little stuffed animals and "'Marlowe,'" she says; she means my new screen name. "What kind of a name is that?"

"You know," reaching backhanded for my Coke. TV noise echoes down the hallway: Carma's mom and little sister, watching *Off Limits* in the family room. Carma's mom makes her keep the bedroom door cracked when I'm over: *Nothing against Kit but he is a boy, Carmen.* Uh-huh. "Like the playwright. Christopher Marlowe?" Actually my real birth certificate name is Christopher, but I've always been Kit.

"*Playwright*, ooh. You've been reading books

again. . . . Wait, I got it," FAULKNER FORENSICS: THE GREAT DEBATE! and there he is, sky-blue shirt and a tie, wow, leaning over a podium, making some devastating point and "Look how short his hair is there," Carma says, squinting at the screen; she needs glasses big-time, but she won't admit it. "I like it better now that he's growing it out."

"So do I."

"So why didn't you talk to him?" she asks, making the picture bigger, filling half the screen with his face. Those brown, brown eyes. "He was standing right there at the concession stand, why didn't you just—"

"I did talk to him, I said—"

"Sorry. 'Hi, Pablo,' doesn't count."

"Well, what do you want me to do? Go up to him and say, 'Hey there, Pablo, you don't really know me but I've been in love with you since last summer'?"

Last summer: driving past the tennis courts, the buttery high noon light, the car in front of me stopped short, so I stopped. And I saw him. Shirt off and sweating, brown and laughing, yelling across the net: the sun on him. He was the sun. It was like my heart was in my eyes and all of me just, just flew out to him, flew and stuck. I don't even remember driving home. . . . I knew him, I mean I knew who he was from school, how could I not? But I'd never— seen him before.

"Well what *are* you going to do, then? Join the debate team? Keep hanging out at the jazz concerts, and hope he notices you? Phhh," in disgust, to her it's so easy, to her it's just me being a dupe. Like it's all a romance movie or something, our eyes meet across a crowded auditorium, the violins go dah-dah-*dah* and we're off to the sunset hand in hand. . . . Of course I want that too, of course I— But it's not just getting him to notice me, or like me, or whatever. It's like *gay* is a room, and everything—who I love, who I am, the world, sex, everything—is in that room. And before anything else can happen I have to open the door, and walk in.

Carma thinks it should be easy, *just do it, just come out* but she doesn't understand, even Carma doesn't understand. Like that one-in-ten experiment she showed me, where in this school in Maryland or somewhere the GSA, the gay-straight alliance group, snuck in overnight and tagged every tenth thing—lockers, desks, bathroom stalls, trays in the cafeteria, everything they could get their hands on—tagged it all with this little sticker that said TEN PERCENT, like one in ten people are gay, right? And Carma read about this and she was just on fire, *come on we've gotta do it!* She'd like us to do lots of things, but it's not her, right? It's me.

And I could turn it around, couldn't I, and say, *Well where's* your *boyfriend?* She's straight, for god's sake, for her it should be easy. But I don't say that, I don't say anything, I just sit there looking at the screen, those brown eyes and long lashes, the little smile-crease in the corners, the way he looked at the movies when he smiled at his friend, Joel Caspar who plays in the jazz band, too, buying the mega-jumbo popcorn—just a friend, I think. But—

even though Pablo's out, maybe Joel isn't? so maybe they are a couple, secretly? or maybe Joel's gay but they're still just friends? Or maybe Joel's straight and they're just friends?

This whole thing is so confusing.

Now I sigh, and lean back eyes-closed on the bed—there *is* a bed, under all the rumpled sweatshirts and piled blankets and pillows, it's sort of like a hamster habitat—and "Send me the link, OK?" but she doesn't answer, I can feel her staring at me so I open my eyes and "What?" because she's got this very Carma look on her face, sad and mad and something else and "How long," she says, "are you going to look at pictures, Kit? You can do that your whole life, you know."

She looks at me; I look at her. Down the hallway, the TV chatters; her mother and sister laugh.

8

"—mineral water. . . . Lindsay! I'm talking to you!"

The daily broadcast from Planet Bitch: my mother. "What?" at the dining room table, flipping through my mail: college after college, *Unparalled Excellence*, *Go Where You Belong!* and "I asked you," across the table now, hands on the back of a chair, "if Rosa was here today. I told her to pick up some mineral water, and we're all out."

"I just got home," which is a lie, but so what? She just got home herself, she won't know. Anyway Rosa's her problem, not mine. "I didn't see her."

She squeezes down on the chair back like she's in mortal pain. You know, she can get her face done every month if she wants, but those hands just keep saying *old*: bunchy knuckles, shiny skin, and all those stupid rings, her big gaudy trophy rocks. "Did Allen call?"

"I don't know." Allen's her boss. "I didn't check the messages."

She gives this little hissy sigh, like once again I've disappointed her, what else is new? and stomps off for the phone. In five seconds she's back, arms crossed: "Blake called for you. Twice."

A guy and a girl strolling through some Ivy campus, gray stone, red-and-gold autumn leaves: *Be Everything You Are.* The sun slants through the French doors like some tech effect in a play. I don't say anything.

"Are you even going to listen to the messages? He could barely talk, he was so upset."

"Oh boo hoo." He was probably drunk. That's what he does when he gets mad: he gets drunk. Which is why my cell was off. "Don't worry, he'll get over it."

"That's you all over, Lindsay. Hard as nails." She says it like it makes her happy. "You don't deserve a nice boyfriend like Blake."

Nice, right. What would you say, Mom, if I told you what Blake likes to do to me in the Jacuzzi? She'd probably faint. No, she'd probably ask me for his number. . . . Anyway "What difference does it make to you? I can manage my own social life," as I toss the envelope down, it's not what I want, what I need, what do I need? Not Mommy dearest going on and on about how selfish and unfeeling I am; not stupid Blake how I'll probably run into at the sugar party tonight; not—

"—all this noise," from my dad, frowning, I didn't hear him come in. "Jesus, Diane, I can hear you from the hall. —Hi, Lindy."

"Hi, Daddy."

"She won't return her phone calls," my mother says to him, like this is some big crime. "That poor Blake keeps calling and calling, and she—"

"I'm sure Lindy knows what she's doing." I don't think he remembers who Blake is, but I smile anyway. "When's your next show, baby?"

"December 16th."

"I'll put it in my book. Having fun at rehearsals?"

"Lots."

"Good. —Did Rosa pick up my shirts?"

"That's another thing," my mother says, as I step past her. "There's no mineral water, and I specifically *told*—"

—like I specifically told Ashley to pick me up at ten, now it's quarter after and here's Liz instead in the driveway, I hate riding in Liz's smelly ashtray car but "Ashley said she called you," Liz says. She's wearing that white corduroy jacket again, it makes her look like a whale. "She said she had to do some stuff first, and then she'd meet us," at Kelly's, Kelly Onowae, her parents are in Bali or something so everybody's here: in the crush and heat, the music up loud like a club but we're still dancing in somebody's living room, getting high on the terrace, *look at the lights, wow*. Yeah. Wow. The same things we've done, I've done, a million times before.

I remember when I first started going to parties, like back in eighth grade, I thought they were so—I don't know, cool or exciting or something. Everybody was there, the lights were off, the music was loud—and the next day at school you'd talk about it, you know, who did what to who, who got high, and all the people who weren't invited, you knew they were listening, and thinking *Oh god I wish I was there*. But now it's just—

"Hi, Lindsay!" Kelly Onowae, all shiny-eyed from sugar, sweaty from dancing, breathing right into my face. "You made it!"

"Yeah." I wonder what kinds of parties Kit goes to? Kit and what's her name, Carmen Jaworsky? Wonder what they're doing tonight? and "How come you didn't go to Bali with your parents?" I ask Kelly, but she's not even listening, she's reeling away, past the bottles clustered on the table, so I get a drink, a vodka-and-cherry because what else is there to do? I don't like sugar, it gives me a headache, and it makes my face puffy the next day.

So I drink, and I dance with Kwame Moore, and Jason Degirno, two more Blakes, and ignore the real Blake who's already so drunk when he gets there that he spends most of his time puking in the downstairs john. Real sexy, huh? Who wouldn't want a guy like that? . . . What did Kit say? *Be Lola for me*; right. Lola wouldn't be caught dead in a place like this.

And when I get tired of drinking, and dancing, and so bored and irritable I can't take it anymore, I dragnet the house for Ashley to drive me home: Ashley who's wearing some guy's Bakeley T-shirt now, dribbling and sniffling, she gets so disgusting when she's loaded.

"I just wanted to *talk* to him, I just—"

"What'd you do with your shirt?"

"—but then he's all over me, and two seconds later he's like, See you. And I—"

How many times do I have to tell her: stay off the coat pile? "Guys are pigs. So what? Get over it."

"You think you know everything." In the dashlight her face is blotchy, her mouth is pinched and tight. "You think you know what's going on. But you don't."

"I know enough not to get disgusting. . . . Don't pick me up tomorrow," as she slews into my driveway way too fast, just missing my mother's car. The fresh air smells so good, after the stale cherry reek of her breath, her car, my clothes, the party. "I'll drive myself."

REED But what about before that, in, where was it? (*Makes a show of consulting notes.*) In Barcelona?

LOLA Minneapolis, actually.

REED St. Paul, actually. What were you doing there?

. . . could tell me, I'm sure.

REED But it's what you say that matters here, isn't it. So: were you staying with a man in St. Paul? A friend? Or a lover?

. . . germane.

REED (*smiling; it takes a certain effort*) Germane: yes. All your actions, your decisions, your—passions, let's say, are germane to your politics: they're the fertile ground where convictions grow. The wet and slippery mulch. . . . So answer the question. Was Herron your lover?

. . . him. Or have you already?

REED Unfortunately, no. He's unavailable to me.

. . . mean he's dead?

REED What difference would it make to you? To *you*, Lola? Would you miss him? Would you *cry*? (*Comes around to her side of the table, squats beside the stool.*) Were you two comrades, partners in arms, or is it his arms you miss? his kiss? Was he a man to you? Tell me. (LOLA *gazes at him. He whispers.*) *Tell me.*

. . . what we do, or did? What difference would it make to *you*?

(*Silence. He straddles her legs on the stool, hands braced on either side of the seat; his face is an inch from hers, they can feel each other's breath.*)

REED Because I need to know.
All.
About you.

9

Hand-claps sharp as a pistol shot, *one two* and "People," Mick says, stage right and stalking forward, "hold it right there a minute," with me practically on top of Lindsay, so I stop, take a breath, get ready to do the lines again. —You'd think it would get boring, doing scenes over and over, repeating the same words. But it's really not, it's more like, like panning for gold, you do it twenty times and you finally maybe get something great. Unless you get it the first time, like at read-through, that lightning flash. Now I know that those times don't happen often, and you can't make them; but I don't mind. Now it's like fitting a jigsaw puzzle together, *this* piece goes to *this* piece, I trust that there's one big picture so I just keep gathering the pieces.

Like this scene. At first it was just *I need to know!*

All! About you! with me looming over Lindsay like a vampire or something, a cliché villain, she's got this weird look on her face and it's all I can do not to crack up laughing. But then after we did it four or five or a million times, I thought, wait a minute. Reed, he wants Lola, right? Not just as a victory, to make her tell about the resistance movement, but really *wants* her. The same way I want Pablo. And then it was easy.

Lindsay still had trouble, though: she kept messing up lines, which isn't like her. *She* isn't like her, today she's all, I don't know, distracted or wound up or something. Maybe it's because of what's-his-name, Blake, who quit the play and then came back and now just slumps in the back row like a gorilla escaped from the zoo, glaring at her, at me too when we're in our all-about-you clinch, I hope he can tell the difference between a play and real life—

"—very important to say to you. About our performance." Mick frowns, crosses his arms: I feel a long speech coming on so I lean back on my heels, ready to stand up—but Lindsay puts her hand on my arm, stops me where I am; why? It's not like this is comfortable, my right foot's falling asleep. But I can't get away without making a big deal out of it, everyone will look. So I stay where I am.

"You guys may have heard," says Mick, "there's already been some controversy. Certain people—no, I won't name names, but you can probably figure out who they are— these people don't think you're mature enough to handle a play of this nature. Not only the political theme, the terrorism stuff, but the overt—tension between the leads."

In the silence past the stage, someone makes a little sound.

"Maybe," rubbing his chin, "it's because they're threatened. By your skill and commitment, or by their own—no, I shouldn't say that. I can't speak for the administration, god knows. *Or* the school board. But I do know that they think—they've already suggested—that we'd be better off doing something a little less . . . challenging."

"Like what?" Lindsay says, loud. *"You're a Good Man, Charlie Brown?"* A ripple of laughter from the dark, brief and uncertain and "The point is," Mick says, "I have to go on the offensive here, I have to step up to the plate. So my question to you is: Are you behind me in this, people? If things go south. How far are you willing to go?"

South how? what's he really saying? but suddenly Lindsay grabs my hand: hers is warm, and strangely small, I guess after Carma's paw most girls' hands would feel small and "All the way," she says, defiant, like she's making a stand, like she's Lola for real. "Right, Kit?" so what else can I do but squeeze back and say "Yeah," and try to sound like I mean it; I do mean it, I mean it's a great play and I really want to do it, I love acting. But mostly I don't understand.

Then when rehearsal's over, people picking up backpacks and coats, Carma waiting for me on the stage stairs, digging keys from her purse, but "Come on," Mick says to Lindsay and me, leading us backstage, past the dressing rooms, down the dogleg hall to his office. But when we get there the phone's ringing, so he holds up a finger, *one sec-*

ond, and we wait outside, I wait for Lindsay to talk but she doesn't, just stands quiet, head to one side, like a pose, almost. Maybe that's how it is when you're really an actor, you just assume somebody's always watching.

From the other direction, scene shop, we can hear crew, a loud hollow bang and then a laugh, somebody yells "Safety hazard!" and *"You're* the safety hazard, gimme that drill!" and "This is me," Lindsay says, tapping the wall, what does she mean? but then I look closer through the ghost-light dimness, and see the graffiti, blue pink red Magic Marker, words and hearts and a million exclamation points, HH HH No More Extras!!! XXOO JIMMEE!!! ♥ ♥ ♥ Queen of the Dollhouse ♥ ♥ ♥ with her pink fingernail in underline and "From last year," she says. "*A Doll's House*, I was Nora. Didn't you see it?"

Carma was assistant stage manager for *A Doll's House*. She couldn't say enough bad stuff about Lindsay, *prima donna, queen bitch* so "No," I say, trying to look like I wished I had, "I was—" was home, doing what? Reading *Cog* online? With my rich social life, who can remember?

"This is me, too"—LOVE YA LADY LINDSAY!—"and here, and here," her name scratched and scrawled all over this wall that's like one big giant yearbook, I see dates from three years ago, seven, ten, it goes over my head, do they stand on ladders to write or what?

And then just past her pointing hand I see it, Nicely-Nicely Pablo Baby! in Day-Glo orange, my Pablo? so "Is that about, um, Pablo Roy?" I ask, trying to sound nonchalant. "Was he in a play, or—"

"*Guys and Dolls*," she says. "I didn't audition, I was going to Cancún. . . . Don't you know Pablo? He was so fun at Harvest last year. We danced almost every dance, he's so amazing." Head to one side again, a tilted kind of smile. "Did you go to Harvest?"

Dancing with Pablo, what would that be like? *Pablo baby.* "No."

"You mean you didn't take what's-her-name? your girl-friend?"

"Carma, you mean? She's not my girlfriend—" as the door swings open, "Come on in," to Mick in his roll-ing director's chair, Stratford and BAM posters, a huge scribbled-over calendar, comedy-and-tragedy screensaver, one sky-blue face blending, morphing into the other, over and over and "Sit down," he says, reaching to close the door. Lindsay raises her eyebrows at me, perches on the edge of the desk. I can't find anywhere to sit so I stand with my back to the wall, trying not to knock anything down.

"Listen," Mick says, "this is something you guys need to know. But keep it quiet, OK?" A swift sigh, like he's really tired, he swivels again to face us and I see he *is* tired, dry eyes, he squints then opens wide, not groomed stubble but the real thing and "There's going to be a battle here," he says, "about this production. We've got some support in the school, the Lit teachers in particular—I did a huge presentation for them, I really—anyway. Some other peo-ple—parents, mainly—are complaining to Mr. Deakins"—he's the principal—"and the school board. Pretty serious complaints."

"Like what?" Lindsay asks, frowning.

"They think the play's way too political, for one thing. The whole terrorist/freedom fighter business. One parent asked if it was supposed to be about Palestine. . . . And they think the scenes with you two are 'inappropriate.' By which I guess they mean the sexual tension between the characters."

"*So?*" really shitty.

"So Mr. Deakins is coming to rehearsal. To 'observe.'" He's smiling when he says it, a weary little smile and like a kaleidoscope clicking, new picture, I see Mick not as a teacher, Herr Direktor, but a person, a guy not a whole lot older than we are, trying to figure out a way to do what he wants to do, has to do and "What about you?" I say. "Could you get in trouble, or something?"

He shrugs; he doesn't look at me. "Could be. I don't know. Drama's not strictly academics, even at a school like this, so— Anyway. That's not your problem. But I meant what I said, out there," gesturing back to the door, the stage. "If I go to the wall, I have to know that you're be-hind me. You two in particular, since you're the heart of the piece. Otherwise there's no point. So what do you say? When the shit hits the fan, are you going to run?"

"What can they do to me?" Lindsay says. "I'm a senior. I don't care."

"Kit?"

Well, what can they do? call me names? run me out of town? and in my mind my mother's voice: *The idea behind the play, that the self is revealed no matter what*—that's *threatening*. Threatening to who? Mr. Deakins? the school board? *Because what people want is for other people to think that they're good, to* believe *that they're good and not the way they really are: greedy, angry, and scared. Scared most of all* and "I'm not scared," I say. "It's a great play, I want to do it," and Lindsay smiles, a truly pretty smile, you can see what guys might see in her and "All right," Mick says, and slaps the arms of his chair. "Then I'll slay my dragon. —Remember, keep this just between us," so out we go, down the hall that smells pleasantly of dust and old paint and makeup, walking side by side without saying anything, like comrades, until "I'm going to the Galleria," Lindsay says, hitching her purse up her shoulder. "Want to come?"

The Galleria? and do what? Shop? but when I don't answer right away she smiles that smile again, so sweet and "We could talk," she says. "About, you know, the play and everything," but "I can't," I say, glad it's not a lie. "I'm going out with Carma, she's waiting for me now."

Her smile changes, morphs like the comedy-and-tragedy masks, she starts to say something but "Kit," Carma yells from down the hall, and someone's with her, Jefrey-with-one-F. Again. "Kit, come *on!*" so "I have to go," I say to Lindsay, scoop my bag from Carma's arms, follow her and Jef to the parking lot where gorilla Blake is leaning on his silver Jeep, he stares at us, at me? as we pass and "Uh-oh," says Carma cheerily, jangling her keys, "looks like Bluto's picked up your scent. Throw him a chew-toy, quick. . . . We're giving Jef a ride, OK?"

Jef hops into the backseat, forest of little braids bobbing: "Where you guys headed?" but I don't want her to answer, to say *Oh we're going to some café to stalk Pablo, want to come along?* so "What'd you think," I jump in quick, "about what Mick said? About the, the controversy and all that?"

Carma palms the wheel hard, her usual race car style. "I think it's bullshit. Somebody's got a grudge or something, maybe somebody who didn't get a part—"

"I think it's fascist, plain and simple," says Jef. He's leaning forward on the seat, his voice right in my ear; a smell like oranges, and clean skin. "Who are they to say what kind of play we can put on? Carm, remember when we did *Anne Frank*?" and they go off on that, memory lane as we barrel into traffic, past Bib's, past 7-Eleven, take the long turn onto Shore Drive and all the while I'm thinking of what Lindsay said, of dancing with Pablo, *he's so amazing*; yeah. The way he gestures when he makes a debate point, that little two-finger shake; the way he walks down the hall, saying hi to everybody, teachers, freshmen, everybody; the way he peeks over his sunglasses, gold lenses that make his brown eyes glow—

"—Kit? Yoo-hoo, try to pay attention," and we're in a driveway, Jef's face pink as he leans in the window: "No no, I'll just, I'll see you guys tomorrow— Bye, Kit," and then gone up the driveway, red-and-brown slurry of fallen leaves, black-and-white dog barking happy in the yard.

"What is it with you today?" Carma says as we roar off, gravel scatter, her sharp sideways frown. "First you're hanging tight with the Bitch Queen, then when poor Jef tries his best to talk to you, you're—"

"I wasn't 'hanging tight' with her. We were in Mick's office, he called us in—"

"You were in the hall together, I saw you. . . . So what did she say? What were you guys talking about?"

"Nothing. Just—Pablo."

"*Pablo*? What about him? What'd she say?"

What are you, a cop? my keeper? so I don't answer at first, watch the rosaries dangle and sway, bright beads like jewels of captured light and "She said," staring out the window, stop-and-go flow of buildings, street signs and traffic and trees, "that he's an amazing dancer."

"Wow, breaking news. She spends a whole night in the gym with him and that's the best she can do? —Do you know where this place is, by the way?" *this place* meaning where we're headed, café grand opening, Tropic of Coffee, where it takes her ten unending minutes to find a parking place, by the time we get inside the trio's already done and packing up, Pablo in a FAULKNER JAZZ sweatshirt joking with Joel Caspar and the girl who plays clarinet, "Great set!" and "Go on," Carma right in my ear, like a cartoon angel, devil, on your shoulder, which one is she? "Go say something to him."

"Carma—"

"I mean it. Or I will. 'Hi, Pablo, this is Kit, he's in love with you—'"

"Carma, shut up!" too loud, a couple heads turn but not his, he's snapping shut his trumpet case, some guy in a shirt and tie is handing him a T-shirt, billowy blue, ugly sketchy palm tree above a coffee cup: "—many thanks for your fine music," and Pablo smiles, that wide sunny smile, like in all the world this T-shirt is the thing he wants most—

—and in the light of that smile, that, that *ease*, what can I say? Like he's a big open room and I'm a small cramped closet, closet, right, but how can I just walk over there, go up to him and say, what? You're where I want to be, who I want to be, who I want—

"—*ridiculous*," Carma's hiss and gone, across the room in two steps, touching his arm and I, I need to hide, I want to run but he's waving at me, a friendly little wave so I have no choice, I have to go over there, stand stiff and smiling like a ventriloquist's dummy while Carma babbles on and on: *oh wow the jazz band gee we love jazz, and coffee too, me and Kit go to Bib's every day, you ever get the mocha crème there?*

—and all the while Pablo's smiling, nodding, like this is an actual conversation between normal people: "Yeah, I go to Bib's sometimes." Up close I see how dark his eyes are, his long strong hands, I can feel myself start to sweat and "Are you going to the play?" Carma says. Her voice is so loud, people turn to look, the T-shirt tie guy, the clarinet girl. "Kit's the star, you know, he's really—"

The clarinet girl—what's her name again? Leah?—leans over and "I heard," she says, "that they're going to cancel the play this time. It's, like, it's too weird or something? Darnell Foster said—"

"*I* heard it's pretty sexy," Pablo says, and grins at me. At me! "You and Lindsay Walsh, huh?" Me and Lindsay? *Sexy*—oh no, oh *shit*, now he thinks—but "Hey," says Joel

Caspar, nudging him, "we gotta get back, Ed needs the van," so "Break a leg," Pablo says, and smiles at me again, picks up his case and he's gone, clarinet girl, Joel Caspar, everybody out the door and Carma's digging for her keys, she says something inane and I don't answer, I don't think I've ever been as mad at her as I am right now.

Finally, almost home and I still won't answer, won't talk at all, just hunch in the seat, my head against the window so she slaps the radio off and "At least he knows your name now!" she says, defensive. "At least now he knows who you are."

"Oh yeah. Kit, the ladies' man."

"Well you could have said something, too, you know, you could have—"

"Like what? 'Excuse me, but I'm a homo'?" I jab the radio back on. "Just leave it alone, all right? You've done enough for one day."

Radio off, her voice is shaking: "Kit, that's not fair! I wanted to help, I tried—"

She *tried*, she's always *trying*, she acts like it's her and not me but "I don't want your help, OK? I never asked for it!" and the radio back on, loud, a song we both hate but no one reaches for the volume, no one says anything, the car's filled with noise but only silence underneath, her car's still rolling up the driveway when I fling the door wide, she roars away and "Good grief," my mother says. On the porch, one hand in the mailbox; I didn't even see she was there. "What's wrong with Carmen?"

"Nothing's wrong with her. She's *fine*," and I try to get

around her even though I know what's coming, some motherly word of comfort, advice, nothing I can stand to hear—

—but she surprises me, she lets me go, watching as I pass, but with my door slammed tight I'm safe, I can sit on the bed and pound my fists into the mattress, punch down with all my strength because there's nothing else to do, it's too late because Carma's right, isn't she? I could have said something, I could have laughed it off, said *Uh-uh* or *Not me* or *Why don't you come to the show, see for yourself?* Or better yet I could have gone up to him alone, I could have said *Great music* or *What an ugly T-shirt* or, or anything, but I didn't, I couldn't, I'll never do anything because all I can do, all I ever do, is watch, right? Just sit in the window seat and *watch*?

Up above me, his smiling face.

Pablo baby.

I pull the covers up to my chin, I close my eyes; but it's no use. I can't fall asleep now, I'm wide-awake.

LOLA But it didn't happen overnight, Your Honor. It's a process. (*Sways on her feet. Two* RUNNERS *flank her, steady her.*) Like the law. Or justice.

THE JUDGE Answer the question you were asked.

LOLA I'm sorry, I'm trying to. I haven't slept for a few days. Your Honor, I—

. . . seat for the defendant.

LOLA (*sits; makes a grimace, tries to hide it. Briefly rubs her bandaged leg.*) Thank you. . . . All right. I became involved with the Freedom Movement—

. . . Resistance.

LOLA (*smiles*) "Resistance" implies opposition. To force. We like to think more positively about our government.

. . . dangerously frivolous. You've rejected the help of your advocate, Mr. Reed—

LOLA I've rejected no one. (*Looks to* REED, *who stands behind the "bars." Their eyes meet.*) I've chosen to represent myself; who better? And I know exactly what this trial is about. Not "sabotage," or a burned building—

. . . indisputable! There were eyewitnesses, Your Honor—

. . . will answer the question.

. . . lies! A raveling, snake's skin river of lies—

. . . out of order, Mr. Reed! (*Gaveling*.) The defendant will answer the question! Truthfully!

LOLA I'm under oath, Your Honor, I can't lie; I won't. About who I am, why I'm here, or what this is about. The bare fact is—and it's as bare as a knife blade, no one knows that better than I—I'm in this room because I'm free.

I am already free.

And you know that, Your Honor, you and the government you represent. All these people, here: they know it too. (*Locks gaze with* REED.) If I wasn't, I wouldn't be here at all, would I?

THE JUDGE Escort the defendant to chambers.

10

———◆———

The Judge, Alice Metsig, stares at me as the two Runners "escort" me off, Josh Burnett and the other kid, I forget his name, Blake buys sugar from him sometimes. Then she follows stage right, stands beside me in the dimness and "Who's that sitting with Deakins?" she asks, squinting out front. "The Wicked Witch of the West?"

"That's Mrs. Tudor," as in Blake Tudor's mommy, another mummy like my mother, she's got on enough under-eye concealer to face-paint the whole cast. Mrs. Tudor always looks at me like I'm some kind of evil slut, today especially. She watched them drag me off like she wished it was for real. My mother can't stand her either. Last night I overheard her telling my dad: *Angie Tudor—ax to grind—go to the parents' meeting.*

You're saying she could derail the play? Lindy's play?

I'm saying she'll try to, unless we do something about it. Deakins is totally spineless. Although I don't mind the controversy, in a way it does Lindsay a favor, raises the play's profile—maybe even some media interest which is where I stopped listening, I knew what was coming next: *looks good on an application*, college, that's all she ever thinks about. My dad wants me to go to college because he thinks it'll make me happy. My mother wants it because she wants me out of the house.

Now Alice squints into the dark again: "So she's like the queen of the school board, or something?"

"I don't know. Who cares? —*Shhh*," as Kit goes into his "masks" speech, it's my favorite thing he does in the play, almost, except for our last scene together, and the one where he sits on my legs. . . . He's watched me get hauled away—we won't be together again onstage until the fire scene—and he's realizing that there's nothing he can do, legally, to save me. But if he steps outside the legal system, he'll be an outlaw like me, which turns him into everything he hates. So there are a lot of ways Kit could play it: he could be outraged, he could be all noble and suffering and Shakespeare-y, he could flip out, whatever. But he doesn't do any of that.

What he does is start out flat and still, hands at his sides, just like *Well there she goes, I told her so, it's over*. And then as the speech goes on—*I warned her what happens when you take the mask off*, and all that—he just *stays* in that place, gets flatter and flatter, more and more still, like he's being—squeezed down. Squeezed *in*. And it's incredibly scary to watch, because you're sitting there thinking, When is he going to explode?

But what I don't understand is, how does he know to do this? I mean he's never acted before, how did he *know*? By instinct? It's much easier to play big, what Mick calls calling home, just blowing it out to the back row: and it feels better, too. Like you're expanding, filling up all the space on the stage. But this way, Kit's way, you can totally feel the tension, his whole long body is vibrating with it, and you vibrate, too, just watching. It's—amazing. He's amazing.

And then when he's done—he just walks offstage—no storming away, nothing like that, just walks off and up to where I'm standing and "Wow," Alice Metsig says. She squeezes his arm. "If that doesn't convince them, nothing will."

"Shucks," he whispers back, smiles at her, she's still holding on to his arm so "Kit," I say in his ear—his hair tickles my cheek, he needs a haircut so bad—"I have to talk to you." And I take his other arm, start to tow him away until "People," Mick calls from out front. "People, everybody, onstage. —We're going to end a little early today," he says. "Back to regular time tomorrow," and Mrs. Tudor leans over and says something to Deakins who says something to Mick who doesn't say anything. I'd love to say something to Mrs. Tudor, something like *How's Blake these days?* just to see the look on her face—

—but Kit's already got his coat on, he's heading for the

door and I see what's-her-name, Carmen, standing there watching him, but he never looks back at her. So I call out to him, he stops, and "You want a ride?" I say. And he nods. Simple as that.

So we're in my car, him all scrunched up around his giant backpack, putting on these dumb blue sunglasses that I reach over and take right back off: "I can't see your eyes," and he laughs a little, that little coughing laugh he does when he's embarrassed, or doesn't know what to say; I don't think he does know what to say. It's so cute. Not like Blake and all those other assholes, always ready with some line, some bullshit they got from a movie or something. Everything is different with Kit.

As we pull out of the parking lot he starts giving me directions, the way to his house but I need to get some moisturizer so "We're going to stop at the Galleria first," the Face Shoppe and Preludia and Justine's, he follows me around, not saying much. He doesn't look too happy here, he looks—not exactly out of place, but—I don't know. Not that he's not right for the Galleria, but that it's not right for him.

Anyway we finally end up at Alberto's, they're the only ones who have that black Cuban coffee I love. And I tell him about when I went to Miami, and how the guys called me *bella*, and how the gay guys wore these amazing little red T-shirts, all slashed up to show their muscles. . . . And he's just, just hanging on every word, hands clasped around his coffee cup, and I wonder why I never noticed him before the play, when he's so cute, you know, in his own funny Kit kind of way, those big eyes, and those long fingers. I wonder what he would be like. . . . People would think I was crazy, I'm sure, and Ashley would completely *wet* herself—and Blake, Blake would kill himself, *You left me for him?* which is basically what he said the other day in the Quad, I mean not really but *You want him,* he said, *I can tell,* but that's absolutely none of his business and I told him so, among other things, like where does he get off stalking me in the parking lot, or at parties, or even here, at the Galleria? I saw him walk past Justine's like three times.

If I ever want to talk to you, I told him, *I know your number. Or I can find you in the bathroom, puking.*

So you're not going to Harvest with me? with his face all squashed up and horrible-looking, I can't believe I ever thought he was hot. Next to Kit he looks like a mutant or something. *You're going with that little faggot instead?* which didn't deserve an answer so I didn't give him one, just brushed him off and went back into school, with Ashley following along yammering about how I could at least *talk* to him, he's obviously in pain and blah blah blah and *You sound like my bitch mother,* I told her. *If you're so worried about it, talk to him yourself.*

But I don't want to think about all that now, boring Blake and his boring broken heart which is really his deflated dick, that's all he cares about anyway, he doesn't care about me. So "I heard," I say, topping off my cup, "that Mrs. Tudor wants to shut us down."

Kit swirls his coffee, stares into the cup. "God, I hope not. I love this play, I mean I love doing it."

"Although they maybe have a point," I say, to tease him.

"It does get kind of hot. Like that part where you're like right on top of me"—and I squeeze his hand as he makes a funny little face, and laughs his embarrassed laugh, god he is *cute*. That little wrinkle between his eyes. . . . "But it's a mute point, don't you think?"

"Moot?"

"That's what I said, mute point. Nothing's going to happen. Mrs. Tudor's just pissed because Blake quit the play for good."

"Blake, yeah. Did you see him, when you were in that makeup store? He was out there by the fountain, he—"

"Yes I saw him. He's such an asshole, he's stalking me because I broke up with him." I wait for Kit to say something, but he doesn't. "I should have done it a long time ago. He even got jealous when I went to Harvest last year with Pablo, I mean come *on*, it's not like me and Pablo are going to hop into bed together, right?"

And he turns completely red, oh my god he's actually blushing because we're talking about sex! I can't believe it.

And then he starts saying he has to get home, he's got some stuff to do and "Sure," I say, gathering up my bags. I play the radio all the way back because he doesn't talk at all, his face is closed up tight. Normally I'd say I know what he's thinking, because I *would* know, but with Kit . . .

When we pull up in his driveway—a little driveway, a really little house—there's a guy outside, rumpled khakis and a baseball cap, digging in the flower beds, the gardener I thought but "Hi," he says to Kit and smiles at me and "Hi," Kit dragging out his backpack, half tangled in the straps. "Lindsay, this is my dad. Dad, this is Lindsay. From the play," and his dad smiles wider, leans down to look in my window, he's got that same little wrinkle between his eyes too: "Oh, *Talk*, yes. We're really looking forward to seeing it. Kit tells us it's quite a production."

"He's an amazing actor," I say. "Bet he didn't tell you that."

"No, he didn't, actually. —Nice to meet you," and "Bye," I call to Kit, his dad waves as I pull away, as Kit ducks into the house, his sunglasses left behind on the seat so I put them on, sweet blue glaze, thinking of how he looked when I made him take them off, the way he looked at me across the table, that adorable *blush*. . . . You know what? I think he is going to take me to Harvest. Because I'm going to tell him to.

11

"Take a look at this," as my dad hands me a letter across the table, some college thing? no, it's from school, from Deakins. It's written in a kind of soothing, say-nothing double-talk, about how there've been so many rumors and misconceptions about *the play* that he just wants to set the record straight, he's calling an open meeting, public forum, Mick's going to be there to answer questions but "Not you?" my dad says, with a question mark in his voice, which could mean *You're not going to do this, are you?* or *Why aren't you going to do this?* which is the sideways kind of way my dad always asks questions. It's his lawyer thing.

"I don't know," I say, looking not at him but down, past the letter to the blue swirl pattern of the tablecloth, like looking through my blue sunglasses. Which I lost somewhere. "I have some stuff to do that night," stuff like seeing Pablo play, a jazz concert at the community center, Carma stuck the ticket in my locker yesterday. . . . So we're friends again, I mean we never stopped being friends. But something's still not right, something's between us, filmy and indistinct like a, a scrim, a curtain between how we were and how we are now. But who can you talk to about a problem when your best friend is the problem?

Plus now when I see Pablo in the hall he sees me back, and smiles at me, the same kind of smile he gives to everyone, progress I guess but I know I'm stuck in his mental file as *Kit: actor:* SEE ALSO *Lindsay Walsh*. Does everything in my life have to be shitty all at once?

"Well," says my mom, as she pours another half glass of wine, sunny and clear, "*I* want to go. Someone has to stand up and be the voice of reason, you can't let philistines like Angie Tudor run the whole show. . . . Although I can't say I'm totally happy about you being in this play. —Grades," she says, when I stare. "You're always at rehearsal, you're not keeping up with your homework—Ms. Malden called, she said you're pulling a 64 in Spanish?" *¡y cómo!* "And your Lit teacher says you're missing a major report, a *Clockwork Orange* paper—"

"I turned that in," three days late, true, but I did turn it in. How do they expect me to concentrate on everything all at once? "I love being in the play," I say, as Pixy leaps onto my lap, burrows deep into my napkin: hunting the last shreds of dinner, faint dried speckles of cheese; I set him back down. "I can make up the Spanish."

"School isn't solely academics," says my dad. "And according to Kit's friend Lindsay, he's an 'amazing' actor."

"Well, I'm not surprised, Kit can do anything he sets his heart on." Unless it has to do with Pablo. "And it's a very demanding role, the Reed part. I've read it. —So who's Lindsay?"

My dad arches his eyebrows. "Very pretty blonde. Drove Kit home the other day. She's the other lead, I'm guessing?"

"Oh, she's Lola," my mother says. "Do you like her, Kit?" Like I'm five years old. Yes, Mommy, she's very nice and I like her, and she likes me, I'm starting to think, to hope not, *you and Lindsay Walsh*, oh please no. But then what was all that teasing and hand-holding stuff in the café? And making me stay on her legs in rehearsal? *Right on top of me*, god. This is why I need Carma. This is why I need Pablo. This is why I need to—

"—tell Carmen, eh? She'll be pretty jealous."

"She's had you to herself for so long," and now they're grinning at each other, this dumb *Oh our baby boy is discovering girls!* smile that makes me want to run away, to say *You're wrong, you don't know me, you don't know anything* but I don't, I just sit staring at the tablecloth, dry blue sea that leads nowhere until "Kit," my mother says, very carefully. "Kit? Did we say something wrong?"

Something wrong? No, Mom, I'm the one who's wrong and always will be, the one who's *ugly* and *terrible* and gay gay gay and "No," I say, still staring at the tablecloth. "It's just—I don't like Carma that way. I never have." My voice sounds flat, like I'm reading out lines I don't like but can't avoid. Is this The Talk? Oh god, I never wanted to have The Talk. Why can't it just, just *be*? Every bad family cliché goes through me: *you're no son of mine, evil bad depraved*, I know they won't, they never would, but still, what if they did? I've read about that happening, kids think parents are going to act one way, but then you tell them and they fall apart, they blame you, they throw you out of the house—oh they wouldn't, I don't think they would. But still it's hard to breathe, my chest feels like lead. *You've never acted before, seriously? A very demanding role*. Especially when you play it every day. Straight boy. Closet case. Perfect son.

"She's my friend," I say into the silence. "That's all."

No one says anything. Pixy winds under the table, around my legs; I pick him up; he struggles down again. The hall clock makes its half-hour noise, a wind-chime tinkle, sweet and fragile and gone. My dad clears his throat but it's my mom who says "Kit," keeps saying it until I have to look up: as her gaze takes mine like one hand takes another, holds it close and "You *are* amazing," she says. She's smiling, not big but deep, raindrop ocean; her eyes are very bright. "Don't you think we know that? We've always known that."

My dad says nothing. He's got his lawyer's face on for sure, smooth and calm, giving nothing away, closed door locked from the inside—until he makes a tiny smile, a head shake and "It's no surprise to me," he says, as if he's saying two things at once, the lines behind the lines, what Mick calls the scaffolding. *Walk the scaffolding, people, that's what it's there for!* "You know I'm a bit of an actor myself. In a courtroom you have to be."

"There's a lot of court in the play," I say. Now it's as if we're all saying lines, tossing them back and forth like in rehearsal. "When you see it, you can tell me if we did it right."

"The right way to do it," he says, "is the right way to do anything: full on. No maybes, no half measures. Right?"

"Right," I say.

"Pro bono," my mother says.

And then my dad is reaching for a glass, for the wine bottle, "You want a drop more?" and my mom takes up the letter from Deakins: "So when exactly is this meeting?" and they start talking about censorship and Lawson Shoals and community standards as I push back from the table, relief like a helium wave to carry me: plate to the sink, fill Pixy's water bowl, head up to my room thinking So now they know, or kind of know but don't mind, or if they mind they don't mind *me* and the lead in my chest is gone and I can breathe again, a deep dizzy breath in the glow of the screen, Carma online demanding where have I been and did I get the ticket and did I see that stupid letter, even the crew got letters, *at least Deakins knows we can read*

did you read it

no too stupid. we have 2 go tho. now what about the concert R U going or what???

His face above me on the wall, that poster-boy smile. What would he do if he knew? about me, about how I feel for him? What would *I* do, set free with something bigger than relief—release, into that room where everything is, everything I want?

A different kind of weight in my chest: a heat. Carma's voice remembered: *How long are you just going to look at pictures?*

No maybes, no half measures.

Bright on the screen: *well R you???*

And my fingers on the keyboard, *yeah I'll go. the meeting 1st right?* I'll go up to him, right up to him, and I'll say— something, god I don't know what, but something. Finally. *CU tomorrow.*

12

The auditorium—I can't believe this—is almost half-full, all these parents sitting there droning over the handout Mick wrote up, he had me and Kit look it over at rehearsal: *You two are the play, it affects you more than anyone.* It gives a synopsis, and some kind of, what's it called, bibliography, all these psych books about why theater is good for you. He even wanted us to be onstage with him, like moral support or something, but I said no way am I sitting up there with Mrs. Bitch Tudor.

So instead we're in the front row, me and Kit—and Dan Castle and Alice Metsig, and the freshman kid who plays the Boy, I can never remember his name—*and* Kit's stupid non-girlfriend in her stupid red scrunchy hat, she shouldn't even be here, she's not even in the play. Plus she keeps glancing at me, she thinks I can't see her or something, these nasty little sideways peeks. Who knows what her problem is. . . . Right now my problem is Kit, he's barely said two words to me, just ignores everything and keeps checking his watch, even when "Our leads," Mick says, "Lindsay Walsh and Kit Webster—" and everyone stares, I stand up to give them a good look but Kit just sits there with his hands in his lap, I could slap him, I yank his sleeve hard as Mick goes on: "It's an honor for me to be working with kids as talented and dedicated as these two. And everyone involved, the actors, the crew," as I, we sit down, I give Kit a huge frown but he doesn't even notice, what's *wrong* with him tonight? It's like he's not even here at all. I was going to drive him home after, and talk about Harvest, but now—

"—giving their best to an all-consuming experience like *Talk*. It heartens me, as an educator, to—"

"As a *parent*," says Mrs. Tudor, cutting him off, "what troubles *me* is the content. And the fact that no parent was consulted about the choice in the first place. This—production—deals with political themes that are far too disturbing, too adult for kids this age to handle."

"They're seniors," Mick says. "Most of them. They're—"

"Prison riots, torture—one of the characters is actually killed onstage! Is this the kind of *entertainment* we want our kids to participate in? Is this the kind of thing we want our educational community to sponsor?"

God, she's such a hypocrite. You should see the movies they have at home, all these weird sex movies, war movies,

Blake tried to make me watch some of them once. . . . But Deakins just sits there nodding, arms folded, like she's made a good point and we should probably do *Sound of Music* instead. My mother's right, he is spineless.

If I turn my head I can see my mother, in fact, straight from work in her Elsa Lisa suit and heels, the ice-blue spikes she never lets me borrow, she's up now and into her riff, *wonderful opportunity for our students* and blah blah blah, all the stuff she was saying to my dad the other day, but it sounds good, I'll give her that. People start murmuring to each other, nodding and "I agree," says this kind of messy-looking woman, lots of flyaway hair, when she stands up Kit and Carmen look at each other, do they know her or something? "It *is* an opportunity for our kids, to be able to move beyond the usual pap offered in most programs, and I think we ought to be grateful to the drama department for trying to do something better. Lawson Shoals is an internationally respected writer, an award-winning—"

Mrs. Tudor stands up, like it's her meeting. "How is this proper high school material? How is this kind of *darkness* appropriate for—"

"They did *The Diary of Anne Frank*," someone else calls out. "That's the Holocaust, and you can't get any darker than—"

"Anne Frank is *real history*," Mrs. Tudor snaps. "This is just fiction, this is—"

"Then where," says the messy-haired woman, "are they supposed to meet these ideas? On TV? Or nowhere at all?"

"Maybe *you* don't mind what your kids see, or do. But some of us believe that there are standards, community standards that—"

"Who decides? You?" Now the flyaway woman's getting angry; her cheeks are flushed. Kit checks his watch again and "Are you late for a plane or something?" I whisper to him. "Are you on a *tight schedule*?"

He doesn't answer, just gives me this very intense look, all eyes, I lean close again so my lips are right against his ear, my breath on his skin and "Listen," I whisper. He smells like Jobé deodorant, like his warm fleecy jacket; like Kit. "I want you to come with me after, I want—"

Now it's my mother bellowing: "Are we in some backwater? This is an affluent and sophisticated community, not some—"

"—school's responsibility! Or isn't it? Mr. Deakins, don't you—"

"This is precisely why I called this forum, this is precisely—"

"Look, Diane, just because your daughter's in this play—"

"Just because your son isn't—"

"Order, order, please—"

"Lindsay will do anything to get people to look at her! My son has enough intelligence not to want to act in a snuff play!"

"Please! Some order!" —And that's when the TV people come in, just one camera and a reporter but everyone turns to watch them come up the aisle: my mother smiles,

Mick jumps up, Deakins hurries to the front of the stage and "Please wait *outside*," he says to them, but no one's listening, everyone's talking over everyone else, Kit looks at his fucking watch *again* and "We have a right!" I shout, putting all my force into my voice and when I do that it *carries*, it cuts through the buzz and mumble, the camera swings my way and "Free speech!" again, I'm calling home, I'm *declaiming*. "*Talk* is free speech!"

I grab Kit by the arm, haul him to his feet and now Alice Metsig's up too, Dan Castle and "Free speech!" I cry again and the camera light's shining full on me, shining like the sun, washing everything away in its big white glare and I feel like Lola for real, brave and fierce and invincible, I turn towards the stage and all of a sudden the crew's crowding around me, everyone's yelling "Free speech!" and they're following me; we're taking the stage, Mrs. Tudor tries to block my way but I push right past her, stand front and center, "Free speech!" as Mrs. Tudor yells at Mick who's yelling too, Deakins rushes offstage, the camera light pivots to track him but then swings back, like it has no choice, like there's nowhere else it should, could, wants to be. Except on me.

"*Free speech!*"

RUNNER FOUR Is this it, Doctor? Is this who you want? (*Takes* THE BOY *by the upper arm.*)

THE DOCTOR Bring the boy into the lab. Now.

LOLA No! He's just a child, he doesn't know— (*Strains against the "bars."*) Reed, stop this, you can stop this, even you must see this is wrong!

REED (*pause*) He refuses to talk to us, Lola. It's out of my hands. (*A longer pause, he crosses to where* LOLA *stands. The "bars" stripe his face.*) I intend no harm, I never have, to him, to—you, never. *Never.* I only want you to tell the truth. You can save him, save us both, Lola, it's up to you.

RUNNER FOUR (*mechanical, almost bored*) Come on.

LOLA (*directly to* RUNNER FOUR) You're next! Don't you know that? If you can do it to him (*points at* THE BOY) they can do it to you! And they will! It'll be your body on the barbed wire next, your head on the—

THE DOCTOR Mr. Reed, we don't have time for—

REED Let her talk.

LOLA (*pounding at the "bars"*) What do you think they want the wire for? Yards and yards of it, miles and miles and—my god! It's all about fear, don't you know that? Fear's the real barbed wire, fear's what holds us in, fences us from our desires, from what we know belongs to us.

Their fear. Not ours.

Are you afraid of him (*Points to* THE BOY)? What can he do to hurt you? Oh god, oh my god you're a man, a human being like him, like me, why don't you *listen*? What could they do to you if you just let him go!

THE DOCTOR Mr. Reed, please, I have sixteen more defendants to process—

REED (*to* RUNNER FOUR) Go on. (RUNNER FOUR *pulls* THE BOY *away*, THE DOCTOR *following.* LOLA *slumps behind the "bars."* REED *approaches.*) Why do you do this to yourself? Nothing is what you think it is. Nothing.

LOLA And you know what's true.

REED I know this: you're putting yourself in danger, terrible danger, and it's all for nothing. Up on the barricades, what do you see? What do you think you see?

This world doesn't work the way you think it does, dream love faith worth nothing in the fire, *nothing.* They *burn* people like you, Lola, they cut you to pieces and call it the common good! The barbed wire's there for a reason, a good reason, it's— Because they can't bear what you represent! Because they're afraid!

LOLA Are you afraid? Reed, tell me. Are you afraid?

REED (*pause*) No. But you should be.

LOLA Of what?

REED Of me.

13

I lean my head against the graffiti'd wall, I rub my eyes; dry grit, like ashes, like ground-up bones. I'm so tired, this day has lasted forever already, and it's only twenty to six. Two more hours of rehearsal to go.

From here onstage is an echo, they're blocking the yard scene again, Nick obediently dying over and over until Mick gets what he wants: Deadweight, that's how I want you to fall. *One of the characters is actually killed onstage!* "Actually," right. How can people be so dumb? That whole meeting was a complete farce, everybody came with their minds already made up. Even my mom. Even though she was right. And the TV crew—no matter what Lindsay thinks, all of that just made everything worse.

She's so happy about it, too: seeing herself on TV.

We watched it on Mick's computer, all of us crowding into his office, but Lindsay wanted to see it over and over, after a while she stood there watching it alone, eyes wide, just— rapt. Carma says Lindsay's mother's the one who called the TV station and tipped them to the meeting, residents divided over local school controversy, *so they could come in and film Evita up there yelling "Free speech!" for her application reel.*

Well, she's right, isn't she? It is *a free speech thing, isn't it?*

Right or wrong she's still a bitch, but without her usual spite, she's tired, too, Carma, and all on edge: about the play, about everything. Me, too. I couldn't sleep after what happened, I'm just walking around like a zombie, dead from the inside out. No point in thinking about it anymore, about Pablo, I want to stop but I can't break the loop, the instant replay that just goes on and on, a snake eating its tail, beginning again as I'm . . .

. . . Ducking away from Lindsay, out of the chaos onstage, rushing through the backstage dark and out to Carma's car, thinking *Finally, finally, tonight I'm going to do it, talk to him, say*—I didn't know what I was going to say but I knew I finally was ready, *no maybes, no half measures, right?* Right.

Fear's the real barbed wire.

And Carma encouraging me all the way, cheering me on, *You know Pablo doesn't have a steady boyfriend since he broke up with that drummer kid, what's his name, Jackson*—and the concert still going as we got there, JAZZ AT THE CENTER, Carma screeching into the parking lot, me leaping out to lope in—

—and see Pablo up there playing, black shirt and glossy red tie, golden trumpet, golden smile. Seeing him took my breath away, took every word I thought to say and turned it to liquid heat in my throat, my heart, I could have laughed or cried or, or anything. Anything at all.

What I did was stand there waiting, vibrating, my pulse like a ragged drum, Carma somewhere in the crowd behind like we'd agreed—*I'll wait for you until, until you don't want me to*—and I thought of how she'd hugged me before I jumped out, warm fierce stranglehold like I was going off to war. Or heaven. Or both.

It *was* like both, my heart was pounding, watching Pablo glance into the audience, checking for someone? and my fantasy that it was me, that dark sweet gaze hunting mine, wanting to find me, see me, know that I was there—

—and just then, just that second he *saw* me, our eyes met and he smiled, dipped his trumpet an inch: to me, to *me*

—as I edged closer, magnet-pulled right in front of the stage, ringed by a crowd not huge but big enough, big and warm as a restless animal and the room so hot I was sweating already, sweaty and stinky and alive, so alive, so *ready* that when he, they, finished the song I was right *there*, I didn't even wait for him to talk first, I got right in front of him and *Pablo, hey*, I said. *Great set.*

Thanks. He was sweating, too, clean sheen in the lights, forehead and upper lip, if I kissed him I would taste it, salt and water and the scent of his skin and *You want a drink or something?* I said, as if it was part of a script, I had no idea where the words came from. I led him—led him!—away from the stage, through the maze of the crowd but then he had to show me, turn me—his hand on my arm, he touched me—to point towards the concession stand, soda and bottled water, I bought one of each, my hands were shaking as I paid; did he see? Did he know I was feeling the echo of his touch, like that part of my arm was glowing, burning, come to life? What would it be like if he touched all of me? all over?

And he was talking, loud to me through the crush, as people kept coming up to him—*Great set!*—and shook his hand, he smiled at them all—and then *Here by yourself?* he asked. *Not with Lindsay?*

SEE ALSO *Lindsay Walsh*, oh no, not anymore. Go on, do it. Do it now! *No. Not with Lindsay. I'm not with her, I don't want her—*

Looking over my shoulder, looking for someone? *Oh right, that other girl, that crew babe's your girlfriend, right?*

No. I don't have a girlfriend. I don't want a—

—but he was still talking, grinning, checking over my shoulder again: *Better look out for that big gorilla, that Blake Tudor, right? Got to use some martial arts on that boy!* laughing, inviting me to laugh, too, so I smiled but *I don't care about all that,* I said, my heart in my mouth, in my eyes, I was going to say it, I *was* saying it, *I want to—*

Yo Pablo!

Black T-shirt, biceps and short blond hair: and Pablo lighting up like a, a supernova, eyes closed and glowing over his shoulder as they hugged, a long, endless, horrible hug, until at last the guy stepped back and noticed me, hand out as Pablo introduced us: *Marc, this is Kit* and *You a musician, too?* the blond asked. Warm grip, older, college for sure: twenty, twenty-one. *Come to hear Miles Junior here?* and Pablo telling him no, *Kit's an actor, he's a lead in the play at school,* and *They do plays here, too,* the blond said. *Fran Colita puts them on, you know her? She's a hell of a producer.*

No, I said, I don't know what I said, I just stood there smiling a fake polite interested smile, an actor's smile, nothing I could say to that hand on his shoulder, that utter blond perfection, Pablo leaning into him, how could I ever compete with that? Even if I was out, even if I—

I have to get going, I finally said. My fake-smiling face felt like it was made out of putty, warm and dead at the same time. *The play. You know.*

Break a leg, said the blond, his hand on Pablo's shoulder, massaging him a little, without thinking, like he did it all the time.

See you later, Pablo said.

And then I was gone, back into the crowd like wading through freezing water, numb all over, so numb I didn't even flinch when I saw Carma see me, watched her hopeful face collapse like a building falling, crumbling to dust but she didn't say a word, then or in the car, just drove me home with the radio on low, my head against the window, my breath fogging the glass, thinking When will the numbness wear off, when will it start to really hurt? tonight? tomorrow? the next second? until *Watch the news*, she said at last, pulling into my driveway, slow and sedate. Like a funeral procession. *You're probably on it.*

No thanks, I said, and got out, I knew she wanted to say more, wants to say it still, her eyes all pink today but what good will talking do, crying, what good will any of it do now? Even if I had said something—and now I'm glad I didn't, so so glad, what if I'd been right in the middle of my big speech when Mr. Perfect walked up? Who *wouldn't* rather have him than me? Who wouldn't—

Stop thinking, I order myself, and pinch the bridge of my nose hard, harder, rub my eyes again as from the scene shop I hear bickering, a muted crash, Carma's shout and some guy's curse, everyone's tense today: like it really is court, like they're waiting for a death-row verdict from Deakins. The school board's meeting right now, in "special session," *Oh big deal* Lindsay's sneer but it *is* a big deal, Mick says they can shut us down if they want to: *Angie Tudor and her cronies, just because your son's not in the play,* is that really what's behind all this community-standards crap? Lindsay says Mrs. Tudor hates her guts because of Blake. *Lindsay will do anything to get people to look at her.* Standing in the monitor glow, watching herself over and over. Was she acting then, too, or did she really mean it? Talk *is free speech!*

"Just give me the nail gun, asshole!"

"I told you, I don't have it!"

What if they vote to shut us down? Are we just going to watch them do it, just roll over and go away? Can't we *do* something, protest, or—I knock my head gently against the yearbook wall, *thunk thunk thunk, think think think* in time with my headache, a dry red throb. Tapestry scrawl above and around me, a rolling blur of pink and orange and blueberry-blue, all the shows and all the words and all the names, Lindsay must be on here a million times. Here she is again, a new one, right by my head: LOLA ROCKS!! in runny yellow, right next to KIT + ME♥

KIT + ME♥

Kit and me? *What?* and my first thought is Lindsay, but no, if she wrote it it would say LINDSAY + KIT and she wouldn't do that anyway. Then who the *hell?* KIT + ME♥ with my fingers on the letters, neat black block, as if touching them is touching the hand that wrote them, whose hand? Has Carma seen this? and I pivot, to call the scene shop: "Hey Carm—"

—but just then Mick's voice on the intercom, *Onstage, everybody onstage* where Dan and Nick are waiting, the crew troops in, Lindsay arrives last of all and "Well, that's it," Mick says. His voice is perfectly flat. "I just got the call from Deakins. We're screwed."

"What?" and a general babble, Lindsay pushing up to the front to stand hands on hips and "The school board voted to cancel the production," Mick says. "They said we can put on another play, subject to their approval—"

"Approval?"

"In, what, four weeks? A whole new play—"

"Assholes!"

"—but we can't do *Talk*. The school board feels it's, uh, disruptive," looking at a note in his hand, the back of one of the meeting flyers, *The Role of Theater in Our Lives*. "'Disruptive and inappropriate in an educational setting.' Deakins said he was sorry, and that he hoped we would understand."

"Bullshit," Lindsay says. Her eyes are bright. She's not even mad. "This is all Mrs. Tudor, the big bitch, this is—"

"Lindsay—"

"Well, it is. She hates me, she's always hated me. But so what? It's our play, they can't tell us what to do."

Doesn't she listen? They *can* tell us what to do, that's the whole point. It's their auditorium, their school, their money that pays for the costumes and the lighting and all the rest, they're in control and all we can do is, is sit there and watch, all we can do is—

"What about someplace else?"

My voice, odd and loud: everyone turns to look. I didn't know I was going to say anything. "Why can't we do it someplace else?"

"Like where?" Mick frowns. He's wearing his faded *Angels in America* T-shirt, his hair is greasy, he looks pissed off and weary and drained. "The parking lot?"

"No, the community center. They have a stage, and there's a lady there, Fran Colita—" *hell of a producer*; blond hair, biceps, don't think about it, don't and "I know Fran," says Alice, from her slump in the front row: now she's sitting up straight. "She was one of the teachers at Camp Shakespeare last year, we did *Twelfth Night*—"

"She's OK," Lindsay shrugs. "I worked with her once. Let's do it." Crisp, like now she's decided, and we can all get with the program. Carma's right, she *is* a real bitch sometimes. But if she thinks we can do this, then other people will, too: move the queen bee and the hive will follow, right? and all of a sudden I feel like laughing, not a happy laugh, but I feel—better? No. But I *feel*: that we can do this, that I can do this, that the show, right, will go on. Fuck the school board. It's our show, my show, I'll show Pablo that I may not be perfect and blond and in college but I'm not just Lindsay's crush of the moment, not just another face in the hall, I'm *me*, I'm *Kit* and *I can act*.

14

"The community center?" My mother wrinkles her nose. She's still sipping on her dinner wine, I can smell it from the doorway. "That barely holds three hundred people. Why didn't you ask me first? I could have called Ed Gregory at Art in the Park, they have that lovely big space in the—"

"It's fine," I say, glaring at her. Ever since the meeting she thinks she's involved in this somehow, that it's her thing, too. If my nails weren't wet I'd slam the door.

"Well your director, what's his name, Nick, really should have consulted—"

"His name is Mick. And it's going to work out *fine*," because I've seen the space, and it is. The dressing rooms are ridiculous, and the stage itself is a little cramped, but this isn't a real set-intensive play, they can modify the lights and whatever. And Fran Colita is OK. I wasn't totally happy with her at my Camp Shakespeare, she's got this real sarcastic way of talking, but she'll be all right as a producer. And Mick loves her, he's like wetting himself with gratitude that some other adult is actually on his side.

And Kit—ever since we changed to this new place, Kit is on *fire*. Sometimes you get to a point in rehearsal where people stop acting and start *being*, and now Kit is like that most of the time. It's amazing. Like Mick said before, it's surface tension, a whole world in a bubble. Our world. When we get up there we're just—in another place. Together. The rest of them follow along, and they're not bad—Dan Castle keeps getting better as the Doctor—but it's our place really, mine and Kit's.

I'm so happy there. I don't think I've ever been so happy with a guy. It's like he understands me, like we know what each other is thinking without even having to say.

Meanwhile my mother's still droning away: "—the article in the *Daily*, I made sure to get extra copies," our dumb little local paper but it was still fairly cool, this half-page article above the fold with a color picture of me onstage, and a little picture of the cover of the play, SCHOOL BOARD VETOES TALK. "Angie Tudor comes off like an utter Nazi. And Deakins—"

I finish painting my thumbnail. Coralicious, a stupid name but it's a nice color, like the split inside of a peach. "There was a thing online, too. Mick showed it to us," on some educational theater site, *The Play's the Thing*. Drama teachers from around the country were giving their opinions, should we or shouldn't we be allowed to do the play, my mother gets all happy when I tell her: "Send me the link!" I've already sent it to my dad but I don't tell her that, I don't have time to talk to her now, I have to be at rehearsal at seven-thirty—

—which I'm saying again in two minutes, because there goes the doorbell and here's Ashley and Liz in the hallway, wearing identical X/S jackets, wanting me to go to the Galleria with them: "For formals," Ashley says. She's got this yellowy lipstick on, it looks disgusting. "For Harvest, remember?"

"We never see you anymore," Liz says. She's looking at Ashley, at me, fiddling with her lighter, click on, click off. "You didn't get to the Club Monaco thing, you didn't go to Elsa's party—"

"Those parties are boring. And I'm busy, I'm in the play, remember? Maybe you saw it? On TV? . . . Anyway I'm not going to Harvest."

Ashley sits down on my bed, fluffs her hair back. "Why not? Because you're not Harvest Queen?"

"I was Queen last year, remember?" but this year I didn't bother to run, so Ashley got it, like I thought she would; Blake is King, no surprise there either. Now she must think she's Cinderella or something, she gives Liz this look and "There were two queens last year," she says, and laughs her snarky little mouse-laugh; Liz snickers along. Liz is such a kiss ass. "You and Pablo Roy. . . . So are you turning into a fag hag, Lindsay? Always hanging out with gay guys?"

"What are you talking about?"

"You know. Pablo, and now your friend Kit. He's gay too, isn't he?"

"Have you been talking to Blake?" I say. "In between fucking him? —Oh, you didn't think I knew?" sweetly, my mother calls it my Little Miss Poison voice. Actually I didn't absolutely *know*, but it's a pretty safe guess. Blake will screw anything, especially these days. "Everybody knows, Ashley. Everybody sees you eat my leftovers."

Her face goes blotchy red, like I slapped her or something. I wouldn't mind slapping her, right across that gooey yellow mouth, lying mouth, yelling mouth yelling now "You hurt him! He cared about you, and you dumped him!"

"How is it any of your business? You want Blake, take him, I don't care. But don't you dare spread rumors about Kit, or—"

"Or what?" Liz looks back and forth between us, back and forth, like it's a tennis match or something. Click on, off, on. "You think you run the whole school, you think you—"

"What I think," I say, leaning very very close to her, so close I can smell the gel on her hair, too sweet, too much, "is that you. Should go. Fuck yourself. —And take her with you," as Liz stuffs her lighter in her purse, grabs her keys and "Blake *hates* you," Liz says; she's almost smiling. "Blake and all his friends, he's going to fuck you over, *everybody* hates you now—" as she follows Ashley down the stairs, my mother's in the hallway with her eyebrows up and *"Don't,"* I say to her, don't anything, don't even look at me because I'm already late for rehearsal because of this stupid bullshit, stupid Ashley who's always been jealous of me, stupid Blake who should be grateful I ever spent five minutes with him, why did I ever let him touch me? Why did I even waste my time?

And then I get to the community center which is pitch dark, just the EXIT signs' glow and "Try it again," someone shouts, and the lights burst on, flicker, go out again but not before I see Kit sitting onstage, head down, swinging his legs—

—and he looks so—*good*, he looks like everything I want, I'm down the aisle in five long strides and "Hey," I say in the darkness, I reach and take his hand, warm to my cold, I squeeze his fingers hard and "Lindsay," he says; I can't see his face, but his voice is so kind. "Lindsay, what's the matter?"

And I could just, just cry or something, I mean it's ridiculous but *"Nothing,"* I say, and then the tears come anyway, it's just that I'm so *mad*, so furious at Ashley and Liz and that bastard Blake, how dare they, how *dare* they and "Come over here," Kit says, and together we grope to the seats, our hands still linked, and I tell him everything, how Ashley's such a bitch, all the hateful stuff she said—

"About Pablo? Why?"

"Just to be a shit to me. And you, too. I mean *fag hag*, how dare she call me that, spread rumors like that? And then she said Blake hates me now, he wants to fuck me over. Me! What did I ever do to him? It's his own fault I broke up with him."

He's quiet a minute. Someone yells "Cut it! Cut it!" as the lights rise, and die again, this time to an orangey glow. Then "Well, did you care about Blake at all?" Kit says. His voice is so anxious, so concerned. "Did you—"

"*No.* Never. He was just—I don't know, something to do on the weekends. Someone to buy me stuff," and I laugh a little; he doesn't. Something topples backstage, a hollow metal crash; the lights go on and stay on. Now I can see him, his sweet serious face. "Anyway I'm done with all that, guys like that. Blake's just holding an asshole grudge because I wouldn't go to Harvest with him. . . . I was going to ask you to take me," and I squeeze his hand, like joking but not really, he knows, he squeezes back and "I'm not the guy for that," he says, very positive, and gives me a look, a Kit look, those beautiful eyes.

We're quiet a minute, just sitting, breathing, together, then "What can they do to you?" he says, from that quiet, like we're the only people in the building, in the world. "Blake and Ashley and, and all those guys? You're in a whole different place, right? You're *Lola*, right? So what can they do to you?

"Let it go, Lola. Let it all go."

Lola: only he would think of that, call me that, only Kit would—

"Kiss me," I say, just like that, I didn't even know I was going to say it until I do but then it's so right, so perfect, it's what's supposed to happen next—

—and he does, on the cheek, leaning close then back away and "I think that does it," Mick calls from somewhere behind us, striding down the aisle, he pauses at our row and "Let's go, people," crooking a finger, Kit lets go of my hand and "Remember," he says, rising to his feet. "You're Lola. Remember."

I don't say anything at first, I can't, I'm still feeling that kiss—so gentle and warm, has anyone ever kissed me that way?—but then "Is that what you do?" I ask, bending to gather my purse, my water bottle. "Be Reed?"

And he stops, for just a second, his face goes totally blank—and then he smiles, a kind of rueful smile and "You tell me," he says, but it's like he means something else, I'm not sure what he means but we can't talk anymore, it's time to get to work, get onstage where Mick's waiting with Fran Colita: headscarf, black mohair cardigan, hands in her pockets and "All done emoting?" she says, and Kit smiles, I don't know why, it's none of her business what we were talking about. "Good. Then let's play."

15

"Can you read this?" gesturing at the screen, Carma's making a flyer: SUPPORT FREE SPEECH!!! *TALK!!!* with a little graphic underneath, two traffic-sign-type people with round heads and open mouths, a cascade of letters curling from one to the other but "How's anyone supposed to know it's about the play?" I say, reaching into her desk-chaos for my tea, cold already in its teddy bear mug. We were supposed to be going out for food, I haven't eaten since a bagel at breakfast but Carma wanted to put up flyers on the way, a flyer she was just starting to make, *it'll only take a second to throw it together* but it's been a half hour already and she isn't even ready to print yet, she's still diddling—

"Down here," she says, and plugs in the text, "it tells," about the play, the dates and times of performances, the rally next Saturday, a parking lot support rally at the community center, to go with—or against—the letters to the editor, the screechy e-mail at school, the louder-and-louder debate because everyone's got an opinion, people whose kids don't even go to Faulkner, people who don't have kids, kids who've never seen the inside of Drama Club but "All of a sudden," Carm scathing, "they're all worried about the *lively arts*. Yeah right. Did you read what that one idiot wrote in the *Daily*? 'We must control our children to keep them safe!' It sounds like a line out of the play!"

"Yes. It's stupid. It's also free speech, right? . . . Look, I'm starving. Let's go eat, and then we can come back and—"

"No," staring at the screen, moving the heads a fraction to the right. "Wait a second, I'm almost done."

"Hey Kit?" from the doorway: Carm's little sister Suze, wearing a FAULKNER DRAMA T-shirt and pink ballet tights. She looks like Carma mixed with their mom, blue eyes and Carma's hair, a foot wide and fuzzy and "Hey Kit," shy, "you want to hear my song? I can play 'Silent Night' on the recorder, want to hear?"

Carma frowns. "Go away, munchkin. No one wants to hear your song. —*Go*," thumbing her down the hall, rolling her eyes as Suze flounces away and "What is it with you and straight girls?" she says, moving the heads another fraction to the left. "You're just a regular chick magnet, aren't you. . . . What'd you end up saying to Her Bitchness? I saw you guys in the vestibule, after—"

"Nothing. She just asked for my e-mail." With shining

eyes and a kiss on the cheek, like this was something we were doing now, going to do, what *am* I going to do about Lindsay?—and Pablo, and KIT + ME♥, and maybe Blake, too, he was looking at me very weird today in the Quad, I mean even weirder than normal—but whatever I end up doing, saying, I don't want to hurt Lindsay. She's not a bad person, no matter what Carm thinks. And I know what it's like to want someone you can't have, can never have. . . . But she's so thickheaded, or, or stubborn, I don't know what she is but she only sees what she wants to see, hears what she wants to hear. I mean all that fag hag stuff, good *grief*. And when I told her my screen name, she got it but she didn't: *Marlowe? for Christopher Marlowe, right? Oh, cute. . . . He was gay, wasn't he?* and me nodding, uh-huh, come on Lindsay, you're not dumb! but "OK," Carma says, "that'll have to do. We'll stick some up at Bangkok-to-Go, and that hair salon next door, and Jef can take some back with—"

"Jef? Is he coming with us?"

She hits PRINT, starts digging for her shoes, rooting in the bedside mess and "Yeah," she says, head down and muffled. "He asked what we were doing, and— Why? Don't you like him?"

"No, he's OK." And he is, he's nice. He knows a lot about theater, he's funny, he tells all these backwards knock-knock jokes—to Carma, not to me. He doesn't say a lot to me, just looks, and smiles. "But is he your new sidekick or something? It's like he goes everywhere with us now."

Dig dig dig for the shoe, flyers piling from the printer.

Suze appears again in the doorway, those big blue eyes; I give her a smile and a thumbs-up, and she smiles back then sprints away, pink legs flashing. Everybody, wanting what they can't have. What does Carm want? What do I want? if I can't have Pablo, ever? *never*, like an echo, I haven't talked to him since I saw that blond, just smiled in the hall, friendly, meaningless: like his face on my wall, I tried to take it down but I couldn't, I didn't. It hurts, oh it hurts, but what else is there? Nothing, no one—

"Hey," Carm says as she rises, sneaker in hand, "any leads yet on that graffiti? Did Alice know who might—"

"No." I pull on my fleece jacket. "I asked Nick, too. No one knows."

"Well, *somebody* knows. Somebody wrote it. Somebody who wants you."

Wants me: sure. If they do they're keeping pretty quiet about it, just a scrawl on the wall, maybe it's a mean joke—but she's giving me the heavy Carma eye, expecting an answer, a response so "What about crew?" I say, obedient. "Maybe Jef or somebody saw—"

"There's no way Jef can tell you who wrote that. —Munchkin, I *said* get *out* of here—"

"I just want to *play*! Kit wants to hear me!" and Suze starts tooting the black plastic recorder, fast before Carm can rout her, something that could be "Silent Night": round and breathy, hollow and sweet, even Carm stops to listen as Suze finds and then follows the old melody, hits the high notes, the last notes and breathes them out, *sleep in heavenly peace*—

—and then looks up at us, at me, and smiles, eager eyes as I smile back and "Nice work, baby," Carm fluffing Suze's hair as we pass, flyers in hands, out into darkness and a shifting, rippling wind; last exhalation of autumn, winter finally on its way. The heater in Carm's car smells like dust and old oil. My breath on the window is a melting cloud of white, there and not-there, over and over and over again.

REED Well. She's gone now. Nothing I can do.

Was there ever?

They shouldn't—handle her that way, though. There's no need for violence. For force. Force brings disorder, and disorder brings punishment. That's the way the system works.

Didn't I tell her that? Didn't I warn her?

(*Pause. He crosses to the dock, where* LOLA *was standing; touches the "bars."*)

The mask is there to protect you, that's what I told her; that's what I know. The mask keeps the fire from your face, keeps your flesh safe, keeps who you are in: *in*, impregnable, secure. Inside you can do what you want, think what you please, anything, but—put the raw self outside, without armor, and what happens?

What *happens*, Lola?

(*He turns away.*)

I asked—I *requested* that the Doctor not— She's weak. Physically. Anyone would be, coming from those cells.

I believe in—order. I believe disorder should be contained, should be punished if need be, I believe in the mask. I wear mine: I always have. I have to. Why couldn't she? This community is made by laws, and laws are made by—by desire, the desire not to be . . . consumed. By chaos.

Did you see how she stumbled, there, by the door? I think she hurt her leg. If they hurt her, I'll—I'll speak to the Judge about it. I'll file a brief on her behalf, I can do that. I was her advocate—but she rejected me.

For your own sake, she said.

I warned her what happens when you take the mask off. I *warned* her.

If I file that brief—

He doesn't trust me. The Doctor. The way he looks at me, it's as if he knows what I'm thinking. Lola knows what I'm thinking.

(*Pause.*)

Don't hurt her. That's all I'm asking. Because I can't do this, you understand? Wear it long enough, it becomes your face, who you are, I can't strip myself like that, skin myself, be raw flesh walking naked in the world—I can't. So don't ask me. Don't force me.

(*Turn his back to us.*)

Oh Lola please Lola don't.

16

———◆———

The rally's even more crowded than I thought it would be, the parking lot is overflowing, cars honking, people holding up their handmade signs: FREE SPEECH FOR STUDENTS! or KEEP KIDS SAFE!!!—Mrs. Bitch Tudor's got that one, at the head of her parents' cohort. Tons of Faulkner kids, some from other schools, too, people I know from drama camps, Camp Shakespeare. YouthArts. Fran Colita's here, Mick in a leather jacket, Alice Metsig and Dan Castle, Carmen in her dumb hat, with a flyer taped to the back of her jacket; but no Kit. No Kit! When he told me he wasn't coming, I completely couldn't believe it:

You have to come! This is all about us!

I just don't think it will help.

Of course it will help! SixNews will be there like they were before, my mother's made sure of that, told my father when we left *Keep an eye out for Ellen Jerry* the reporter: I can see her now, posed in front of the community center, the camera's light making her glow. My dad is right down front now, his own camera pointed up here at the platform stage—

—and he sees me see him, and smiles, a smile just for me, and for a second I'm that three-year-old in the fairy-princess gown, like the whole thing is just another one of my shows; I guess in a way it is.

"Go get 'em, Lindy!"

And then Mick's climbing onstage with a mike, he stands with me and Alice and Dan and "Welcome!" he shouts. It's cold out here, but he's sweating. "It's great to see so much support for free speech!"

Cheers, mostly; a nasty little undertow of boos. I throw back my head, let the wind ruffle my hair. *You're Lola. Remember.* I let my gaze go to this one, that one, making eye contact, letting them see me: a girl from my trig class, a kid from drama camp, some guy I don't know, Ashley—

Ashley? What's she doing here? and then I see Blake and I know: Blake and all his asshole friends, and Ashley and Liz in their X/S jackets; Ashley's holding Blake's hand. The King and Queen of Nothing. I make sure she sees me smile, him too, oh I *wish* Kit was here—

"—support the idea this play really represents: freedom." Mick's voice sounds hollow; he's talking too long, people are going to get bored. "We want everyone to come to the performance, and have a chance to make up your own mind. Love it or hate it, but see it for yourself!"

Signs bobbing, waving; Fran Colita holds out her hand for the mike. Ellen Jerry and her crew orbit the crowd, talking to parents, people with signs, but I need her to talk to me, to *see me*—

—so I take the mike, like Lola would, just *take* it and "Free your mind!" I cry: my voice crests like a wave, electric, alive. Lola's voice: my voice: all the same. "Free your *mind*! Don't let stupid people tell you what to think!"

And like a magnet the camera turns to me, Ellen Jerry's pointing, they start moving through the crowd of people yelling at each other, Mrs. Tudor jabbing her sign up and down, Ashley's screaming something, her face all red—

—and Fran Colita snatches the mike away from me, gives me this *look* but I don't care, Ellen Jerry's coming, the camera light is shining like a star—

—but then it jerks, swivels, something's happening off to the side, people pushing, it's hard to see—and then everyone's pushing, roaring, Ellen Jerry's swept away, is it fighting or what? and I crane to see, half off the stage but *"You,"* Fran Colita's bark in my ear, "stay put!" and she's bounding into the mess, the mob, Mick right behind her and "What's happening?" Dan shouts, "what are they doing?" as I jump down, like jumping into surf, surging waves but I can't see anything, Ellen Jerry or the camera crew, just a tumble of people, heaving shoulders and backs—

—and someone grabs my arm, grabs it hard and holds on: Blake. Dirt smears on his coat, little mean eyes.

"Lindsay. Fucking *bitch*."

"What are you doing?" I pull back; he won't let go. "Get your hands off—"

"Big star!" Yelling in my face, the beer smell comes like a wave, he's so drunk he can hardly stand up. "Big *nothing*! Shit! You left me for a little gayboy, Lindsay. Why'd you do that?" And his mouth sags, like a baby's, like he's going to cry or something. "My opposite. My fucking *opposite*, that's what you *want*—"

"Let *go* of me!" but he keeps squeezing my arm, my elbow, even through my coat sleeve it hurts, why doesn't someone stop him? Why isn't anyone *looking*? and "I fixed his ass," swerving from sad back to mad, "his gay punk bitch ass—"

"If you touch Kit—if you go near Kit—"

"I'll go *near* whoever the hell I—"

Ashley comes out of nowhere, hands on his shoulders—"Blake, come *on*!"—hauling him back and away—

—and gone as I stare after him, oh if he touches Kit I'll kill him, I'll *sue* him, I'll—

"Lindy! *Lindy*!"

"Daddy?"

My father appears to bundle me backwards, one arm around me and the camera, the other forcing our way through the crowd, surge and struggle to reach the car and "Did he hurt you?" panting, unlocking the door. "Are you all right?"

"He squeezed my arm. And Kit—oh Daddy, we have to go to Kit's, Blake said—"

"This is practically a riot," backing up; the sound of sirens, now. I see Mick onstage, yelling into the mike; I see a fire truck—a fire truck? and then we're gone, heading towards home, I keep telling him to go to Kit's but he's not listening, he keeps talking about the *disorder*, that's what he's calling it. *All the disorder*. Like Kit's mask speech. *I believe disorder should be contained, should be punished*, oh my god if Blake did anything to Kit—

"Daddy, *listen* to me, turn *left*!" until he finally stops, hears, does what I say, drives to Kit's house where the first thing we see is—

"—the lawn," my father says. He pulls up slowing, staring. "*Look* at the lawn."

Ground-up grass, tire tracks, Jeep tracks; dirt sprayed all over the front of the house; the flower beds destroyed. Blake did this. Blake and his silver Jeep—

I'm out and hammering at the front door, "Kit! Kit?" but then a car pulls up behind ours, his dad's car and "Kit!" a blur, suddenly my eyes are full of tears. "Oh *Kit*," and I throw my arms around him, tight around his neck, and hang on. "The rally, oh my god—everything went crazy, and Blake—Blake *hurt* me, he was drunk, he hurt my arm and then he—"

But Kit unlocks my clasp around him, moves me back and away, one step, and "Oh yeah," he says. "He's a busy guy." His voice is flat. Completely flat, like, like what? Like the masks scene. Like he's going to implode. "We just came from school. Deakins called. He says he has to report it, but he doesn't want to call it a hate crime—"

He's not making sense. "Report what?" What Blake did to me? How would Deakins know? "What do you—"

"*Blake*. He trashed my locker, Lindsay. They don't know for sure how he got in, but— He wrote FAG FAG FAG on everything, he wrecked everything. My dad—"

I can feel my face getting red, flushing, like something catching on fire. My heart is pounding, a hard furious rhythm. "A hate crime, right! Because he hates *me*! First he tries to break my arm, then— Oh god he's such a liar, he'll do *anything* to get at me, he'll—"

"—listening, Lindsay—"

"I am listening!"

"No you're not. I said, he's not lying."

Staring at me from that flat place, flat plain a million miles away, what is he saying? What is he *saying* to me? "You're not gay, Kit, he's just doing this to hurt me—"

Staring at me. A stranger's eyes. "Yes I am."

"No you're not! You're not!"

"Yes I am, Lindsay! I tried to tell you a hundred times, but you don't listen! You don't pay attention to anything but yourself."

Kit's face: no face I know. His eyes.

"*No!*" Why is he looking at me like that? Why is he *doing* this to me? "I *hate* you!" and then into the car, slamming the door with all my might, hands to my face to block it all out, him, all of it, keep it far away from me. . . . I hear the other door open, close; the engine starts.

"Lindy?"

Don't talk to me. Just go.

"Lindy, honey, are you—"

"Just go *home!*" in a voice not mine, nothing is normal, nothing is real. Me, Kit, none of it.

FAG FAG FAG. *Gay punk bitch.*

Fag hag.

Be Lola for me.

No.

17

All the way back from school I kept my mouth shut, tried to hold it in, tried to think, OK, what now? My dad's hands gripping the wheel, baseball cap askew, saying *I think we need to go after this kid* two seconds after he said *I won't do anything you don't want.*

I want it all to go away, Dad. I don't want to get into some giant endless battle with Blake Tudor, it's over, he won, OK? He wanted to get even—never mind that I never did anything to him, let alone steal his girlfriend, good *grief*—but he thinks I did. So he wins: the whole school, the whole world knows, FAG FAG FAG, I'm gay. Hurray. At least he didn't catch me alone somewhere and kick my head in.

But if I do something now, to retaliate, he'll do something else back. Look what he did to the lawn.

. . . And my dad's flowers. Somehow that hurts most of all, seeing those little flowers destroyed. Why? If Blake hates me, fine, whatever. But why wreck things? innocent things?

"—again to Mr. Deakins." My dad is talking in his lawyer voice now, calm, utterly focused. "Your mother and I will be in there tomorrow. You too, if you— Who's that?" frowning as we pull into the drive, a car I don't recognize—but Lindsay's at the door, Lindsay's crying, oh now what? and her drowning clutch around my neck, at first I think she's upset about the, the lawn or something, but then *Blake hurt me* and on and on, well join the club. With her arms around me like I'm supposed to do something about it.

Oh god, Lindsay, I can't help you right now.

"He's a busy guy," and I try to tell her, explain what Blake did, how he and his buddies got into school somehow—they probably hung around after lacrosse practice, that's what the janitors think—and whacked my locker open, just bent the door totally in half. I didn't have much in there, but what there was is history: my old jacket torn to pieces, my spare notebooks, all my books are wrecked, Deakins saying *Of course we'll replace them*, oh gee thanks. *And repaint the wall* over my locker, paint over FAG FAG FAG up there in stinky orange spray paint, the kind they use to make lines on the playing fields, they must have stolen it from the gym—

—and Deakins looking at my dad, not me, never really meeting my eyes: like I'm a leper or something, like I should be as eager to have it painted over as he is, like I should be ashamed—

ugly and terrible

I am not ashamed

—but Lindsay's not listening. As usual. Her father's out of the car now, talking to my dad: they look the same. Not *look* the same—my dad's in his baseball cap and jeans, her dad's in this fancy overstitched coat, leather driving gloves—but their body language, their stance, is the same: protective, angry. Like father bears, or something. Protect the cubs—

—as Lindsay goes on and on, "A hate crime, right! Because he hates *me!*" Oh for god's sake. Does she ever think of anyone but herself? *Ever?*

And so I tell her. Not the way I ever meant to, wanted to, but—I just want her to, to go away. Go away and leave me alone.

"Yes I am," I tell her, and immediately she denies it like she's been denying it for months, backstage, onstage, in the café at the Galleria, everywhere, every time we were together—

"No you're not! You're not!"

—because she wants me to be what *she* wants, needs, not what I *am.* I am gay. I am Kit and I am gay and I don't want to be her boyfriend, I want my own boyfriend, I want to be what I am—

"—Lindsay! I tried to tell you a hundred times, but you don't listen! You don't pay attention to anything but yourself."

And I'm looking at her, staring at her, trying to make her understand but "*No*! I *hate* you!" and then she's jumping into the car, I can see her crying, hands to her face and then her father takes her away, takes her home, my dad and I just stand there and watch them go. Like we're in a movie or something. Finally my dad sighs, not a long sigh but very deep, hissed through his teeth.

"Jesus. Kit, are you all right?"

"I'm fine." My voice sounds weird, very flat and very—flat. I feel like I'm in another world, I *am* in another world, because the world I had is gone. Window seat, safe spectator, FAG FAG FAG for everyone to see. Because everyone will know, everyone in school will know. Pablo, too. "Can I use your car for a little while?"

He looks at me then, a look I've never seen on his face, like—I don't know what it's like. Like he's measuring me, checking some internal list, does he think I'm going to run away from home? crash the car off a bridge? go kick Blake's ass? None of the above, Dad.

Finally "Sure," he says. "I don't know how much gas there is, you might have to put some in."

"OK."

He digs out the keys, hands them to me, looks around the yard and "I'm just glad," he says, "your mother wasn't home."

"Me too."

"Drive carefully," he says.

"I will," and I do, I'm surprised how calm I am, dead calm, driving streets I've driven a million times before—

but not like this, like today, everything's different now. A new world. What kind of world has people like Blake in it, who hate people like me? Gas station, Trader Joe's, Tropic of Coffee, all the way crosstown to Healy, Healy High where Faulkner Forensics is in some competition. I meant to be there for the whole thing—it's why I blew off the rally—but Blake changed my plans.

Walking through the parking lot, hands in my pockets, there's a biggish crowd but I walk right through it, right up to Pablo who's offstage already and drinking a bottle of SmartWater, maybe they're on break or something, maybe it's over and he won—

—and of course there beside him is the blond, Marc, in a gray pullover and jeans, he looks amazing, they both do, they look like people in a magazine and "Hey," I say, because I'm numb, because I can smile, because I don't care. I care so much I can't anymore, does that make sense? and "Hey," again until he sees me, smiles, his friendly public smile, Marc smiles, too and "How's it going?" I say, and they talk, I don't really hear what they're saying, it's loud in there and anyway I'm not listening, I'm looking at Pablo: those eyes, the way his hair gleams under the lights, the way his shirt collar's rubbed a red spot on his neck. *Pablo baby*, dream date, my dream, is that his fault? or mine? But the dream's over so "Here," I say, and dig in my pocket, two tickets, I hand them to him. "Come see me," my nod for Marc, too. "In the play."

"Well thanks," as Marc takes the tickets from Pablo, tucks them in his wallet. "I hear you guys changed venues, eh? So was I right about Fran Colita? Isn't she amazing?"

"Yeah. She is."

Pablo says "Thanks, Kit," and taps me on the shoulder, once-twice, like knocking. Knock knock, who's there? FAG FAG FAG. What will he think when he finds out? Does it matter anymore? "We'll be there. . . . Did you see any of *my* show?" and he and Marc smile, I smile, no I was busy.

"I can't stay," I say. "I have to go."

Pablo nods. "There's like a rally or something today, right? For the play?"

"Right," and I smile, and leave, back through the crowd, back outside in fading sunlight to my dad's car, I try to start it but it stalls, I try again, too much gas, it stalls again and I—

—can't see: hard tears burning under my lids, I squeeze and squeeze but more come out, I can't stop them, I—

can't stand this why is this happening to me I never did anything to anyone I didn't ask for this I just wanted I wanted

to give what I am to find safety to find you

—so I just breathe, breathe, because it's all I can do, breathe in and out and wait: until the tears stop and the gas smell goes and I can start the car, drive home, pull into the driveway where I see my parents, shovel and bucket, trying to fix the flower beds. My mom's been crying, I can see, but she smiles for me; I smile back. No one says anything. There are about fifty messages on the machine, but I don't play any of them; I'm too tired. I take a shower for about an hour, the water as hot as I can stand it, then go to bed.

The next morning I feel the same, not sad or mad, just—there. Numb. My mom asks me if I want to miss school today: Why? What else can they do to me? Brand-new door on my locker, fresh-paint reek, you can't see the words anymore but everybody knows. No one's nasty or anything, but people stop talking when I walk by, watch me as I pass, or in class: FAG FAG FAG. Yes. Or they give me the sympathetic nod, which is somehow almost worse.

At lunchtime Carma says, "Did you give him the tickets?"

"Yeah."

"Is he going to go? With—"

"With his boyfriend. Yeah."

She waits, but I don't say anything else, so "The cops were in to talk to Deakins today. About Blake." Carma sucks her SuperShake. I dip a fry into ketchup, swirl it around, let it drop. I'm not hungry. I have a headache like you wouldn't believe. "I hear Herr Direktor's pressing charges. Or wants to. And Fran said—"

"Can we talk about something else, please?" Across the Quad rain blows in squalls and sheets, gray sleet; almost no one went out to lunch today, the cafeteria is crowded to the walls. Jef threads through like a man in a maze, angling this way, that way, tray in hand, new bandanna bright on his forest-head, flamingo pink-and-orange. He sits down next to Carma, slides the tray across to me: chili dog and curly fries.

"Want some?"

"No thanks."

"Listen," Jef says, then stops, looks at Carma, looks back at me. His voice sounds weird, nervous. Talking to the school victim will do that to a person, I guess. "What happened with Blake—I'm, I'm glad you're out now, Kit. I mean not that it happened like that, and your house and everything, that's really shitty. But—"

"It's OK. I know what you mean."

He and Carma look at each other. "Um, I don't really think you do," Jef says. "Did you read my note?"

"What note?" but he doesn't say, won't say, just starts eating like he's starving and "Fran," says Carma, when no one else will talk, "wants us early today. Crew, I mean. I don't know if it's for cleanup or what. You want to ride with us? me and Jef?"

"No, I'll drive myself."

Across the room I see the crowd of Blake-cronies, and what's-her-name, Ashley, but Blake's not in school today. Maybe he had a hangover or something. Everybody's talking about how drunk he was when he started the fire, backstage at the community center: they threw some stuff around while people were outside making speeches, and burned up a box of props—but not *Talk*'s, they were props for another play, that's how dumb he is. . . . My mom and dad and his mom and dad are meeting with Deakins tonight, but I don't have to be there; anyway I can't. I have to go to rehearsal.

Where I'm a star, of a kind; the wrong kind. Everyone is

so *nice* to me, I wish to hell they'd just forget about it, I wish we could just do the rehearsal. But of course we can't: the phone keeps ringing, Alice starts crying because she missed a line, the lighting board's miscued, everything still stinks in the room that was burned: "—just scorched, really," says Fran Colita on the break; she's got the door closed, so she can smoke. Her office is smaller than Mick's, and even more crowded: piles of old scripts and new flyers, overlapping posters curling on the walls, she's only got one chair, so Mick leans on her desk and I sit on the floor. "If it had really burned, I'd've had that kid's head. Stuffed *and* mounted. . . . The jail props for *Best Western* are a total loss, though."

Mick rubs his eyes. "Listen, I got another call just now from Lindsay's mother. She says she's coming after all."

Lindsay, god. I don't know whether to be relieved or scared. We can't do the play without her, Reed needs Lola, but. . . . I sent her a bunch of e-mails she never answered, and she wasn't in school today. I have no idea what to say when I see her, if she'll even talk to me, especially now that

"She's completely out of control," Mick says. "Her mother says she was up all night crying." He rubs his eyes again. *Cabaret* shirt, wrinkled pants, he looks like he slept in his clothes. Maybe he did. "I'm not entirely sure what her problem is—I guess that Blake kid was her boyfriend, or something?—but is she going to be able to do this?"

No one says anything. I realize he's talking to me. *Can* Lindsay do it, now? With me? I don't know.

"I don't know."

"What about you? After what happened—"

But before I can even open my mouth "Of course he can," Fran says, not like *Sure he can! Boy's a trouper!* but like *One plus one equals two,* like it's a fact, and I know she's right. Because I'm not Reed, after all, am I? Thank you, Blake. I'm Kit, and I can act.

"Sure," I say to Mick, to her. "Don't worry about me."

He lets out a breath. "OK then. When Lindsay gets here, we'll do the fire scene—" and all of a sudden he laughs, a short startled laugh like a bark and then we're all laughing, loud breathless laughter, the fire scene, right, didn't we already do that—

—and it feels good, or at least better, a crack in the layer of numbness, like clean air blowing into a locked room; Fran's laugh turns into a cough and we laugh at *that*, her froggy hack, still chuckling as she swings open the office door—

—to see Lindsay in the hallway, coat still on, hair loose and wet and streaming, like Medusa: she stares at each of us in turn, me the longest

I hate you

and "Big fucking joke," she spits, and walks away.

18

———◆———

Backstage: my place, my world. It always was. But not tonight.

Around me is all the usual pre-show chaos, the mess and flurry I usually love: headsets and throat mikes and the smell of makeup, people scurrying here and there, dropping props and taking deep breaths and running their lines one more time. This place is so tiny, the crowd noise seems to come from everywhere, a whooshing, rumbling, rushing sound; I love that sound, I always have. I used to imagine they were all saying my name, like wave after wave coming into the shore, *Lindsay, Lindsay . . .*

Lindsay, how's your boyfriend? Ashley in the hall yesterday, snickering, with that fat pig Liz. I just ignored her, but a part of me wanted to slap her face off, her ugly face, to yell *Have fun visiting Blake in jail*. I hope he does go to jail, or something, I hope his life is ruined. Mine is, why shouldn't his be?

And why do people keep trying to *talk* to me? Like Jenna, babbling away while she's putting on my makeup, dabbing on the bruises, fluffing my hair—*Oh my god Lindsay it's a totally full house, they're like standing outside to get in!*—but I stared at her in the mirror until she finally got the message and shut up. I don't want to talk to anyone.

Especially not Kit.

He's sitting in my office now, Fran said, *waiting for you*. Right. Wait forever, you *shit*, you shitty little— Because he ruined everything. My *senior play*, ruined. This was supposed to be *my show*.

And it was all going so perfectly, we were perfect together, we could have— But now our bubble world is dead, destroyed. By him. Dress rehearsal yesterday, oh god, I couldn't let him touch me, I felt like I was going to scream. And afterwards Fran tried to talk to me, give me some stupid pep talk about how the show must go on, but I just left, I just could not be there one more second.

He's sent me like twenty e-mails in the last week; I didn't read any of them. I haven't thrown them away yet, I want to, but— When I see him in school I look away. Because I can't stand to look at his face.

Be Lola for me. Oh you *liar*. You weren't Kit for me, were you? You were someone else, someone I don't even know. And I thought—

Now Alice bustles past me in her Judge robes, with two of the Runners, I can't tell which ones in their costumes, helmets with faceplates, uniforms with padded shoulders to make them look bulkier, meaner. Nick the freshman scuttles around in his prison rags, khaki-gray and torn like my prison rags, which tonight don't even seem like mine but just a costume someone put together, something that has nothing to do with me.

For the first time in my entire life, I don't want to go on-stage.

Last night I told my parents I didn't want to do the play; I didn't tell them why. Immediately my mother went off on this huge bitch-out rampage—*You have to, for god's sake, what's wrong with you? Everyone wants to see this play now, Susan Ryder from ACT will be there, Andy Kozlewski, that woman from SixNews, I told her to come! Do you want to make me look stupid?*—which is just her completely, all she ever cares about is herself.

But my dad was just—sad, sitting on the edge of the sofa, looking up at me: *But Lindy, this is your play. What's the problem? Is it that boy?*

That boy. He meant Blake, oh for god's sake why are they so stupid? They don't understand anything, no one does. Except Kit. The old Kit.

Why did this have to happen to me? Why did he *lie*?

I was almost in love with him.

Now Fran's gone onstage, making some kind of thank-you-for-coming speech. Someone touches me on the shoulder, I don't turn but I know it's Mick, I can smell his aftershave, fruity like perfume. Maybe he's gay, too, and not telling anyone.

"Lindsay?" He sounds nervous. "Time."

In the wings, waiting, I can see Kit's shadow, arms folded, head back. What is he thinking of?

Be Lola for me.

No. I won't.

What if I turned to Mick right now and said, *Fuck you?* Let them put on their own stupid play, free speech, what do I care about free speech?

That audience-sound from the darkness, like rushing water, like wind.

Be Lola.

It's your play, Lindy.

For me.

(*Smoke drifts over the stage. The "bars" reflect at a jagged angle, as if they are warped or broken. Offstage we hear shouts and sirens, someone crying or crying out. REED lies facedown, stripped of his bulletproof vest, his left arm at a painful angle. LOLA enters at a trot, looking backward: sees him and comes to a jolting stop.*)

LOLA Oh my god. (*Looks back over her shoulder again, as if pursued.*) Reed— (*She bends closer, reaches with great gentleness to touch his injured arm. Still lying prone, he instantly grabs her leg with his good arm.*)

REED *Got* you.

LOLA Reed! Get up, they're coming. Can you walk? We have to—

REED We're not going anywhere, darling.

LOLA The yard's on fire—oh that poor boy— (*Looks over her shoulder again.*) Hurry, I'll help you.

REED You're not listening. As usual. (*With great emphasis.*) Sit down. (LOLA *reaches for his hand clutching her leg. He yanks at her, swift and brutal, until she loses her balance, and falls to one knee.*) I said. Sit *down.*

It's time for you to listen.

LOLA Let me go—

REED (*hooking his good arm around her neck, dragging her face close to his*) Listen to me. (*Baring his teeth.*) I could kill you, right here, right now. I gave everything for you, don't you see that? Everything I had, I gave. To save you. And what good did it do?

LOLA Stop this! The Runners are—

REED Behind you! (*She starts in fear, tries to rise;* REED *laughs, holds her where she is.*) I thought you were brave. Freedom fighter. Resistance leader—

LOLA I don't want to die. Not here.

> (*The smoke intensifies. The sirens pulse, an eerie, rhythmic sound, like an alien heart.*)

REED I thought *I* was brave. I thought I was alive. (*Coughs.*) Shows what I know. They broke my arm, I think, but that's all right—
> (*Voices offstage, the* RUNNERS, *growing louder.*)
—it was worth it. Worth all of it to give what I am to find safety to find you—

LOLA We have to go. *Now*—

REED (*overlapping*) —Now take this gun, darling (*shakes it from his sleeve into his good hand, offers it to* LOLA), and shoot me. All right? Then you can go. Because I can't go with you, I belong here. But I can't *live* here anymore. So kill me and go.
> (LOLA, *coughing, tries hard to haul him upright. We*

see the shadows of the RUNNERS *through the smoke, very close now.*)

Do I have to kill us both? Or will you do what you have to? what I ask you?

Don't you know I love you?

LOLA If you love me come with me. Reed, Jesus! Get *up*!

(*The* RUNNERS *approach.*)

REED Jesus isn't here, darling. It's all up to you.

(LOLA *sees the* RUNNERS, *looks at* REED; *takes the gun from him and puts it to his head.*)

LOLA (*to the* RUNNERS) Stay where you are or I'll blow his head off.

RUNNER ONE Mr. Reed! Mr. Reed, are you—

LOLA Back off!

(*The* RUNNERS *mill together, unsure what to do.* REED *gazes up at* LOLA *with passionate love.*)

REED Shoot her. Now.

LOLA (*looks at the* RUNNERS, *at* REED; *then smiles, a sudden smile, luminous, almost comic*) Do you want to know my name for you, Reed? I said a long time ago I'd tell you if you asked. (*She puts the gun to her own temple.*) Ask me now, I'll tell you anything.

Let's do it, Reed.
Let's talk.

(*Freeze* LOLA, REED, RUNNERS *in tableau: curtain.*)

END OF PLAY

19

So there we are, in the theater, me and Jef and Carma, waiting for Mick: in the backwash of backstage echoes, doors opening, closing, someone running the floor buffer back and forth, *zzp zzp zzp*. The auditorium smells like dust and ancient makeup, like carpet-cleaner-fake-flower smell: "Ooh, 'Springtime in Hell,'" says Carma, rooting through her backpack. "Here. A pen. It even works. . . . What is *taking* Herr Direktor? I'd like to get out of here today—"

"When is Festival again?"

"March. Read the posters, they're only everywhere."

Festival is Youth Theater Festival, at Crispin University, where *Talk* is going: *Very prestigious, people,* Mick told us, when he passed around the invitation letter. *Very big feather in our cap.*

Did you show it to Mr. Deakins? Alice asked him; he didn't answer, just made a modest little smile. Deakins is still pissed, I guess, that Mick took the play out of the school, so pissed that Mick might not be able to come back to Faulkner next year. I heard him talking about it to Fran, in her office: *I don't care, I'll never regret it, it was one of the highlights of my teaching career. Even if that career's over.*

The smell of menthol; her impatient cough. *Oh for god's sake, stop feeling sorry for yourself. This thing was so much bigger than you.*

Which is how I feel. So much happened to me, because of the play. But it wasn't *about* me, it was like—like getting caught in a tide, or a storm, windstorm that tears at your clothes and hurls dirt in your face and drags you off your feet, and all the while you're trying to hold on and thinking, am I ever going to get through this? And then you do. And where you land—

Now Carma digs out some candy from her backpack, passes it around: CocoChunx, ugh. It tastes like chocolate rubber. "At Festival," she says to me, chewing, "you use their house crew. So me and you," to Jef, "can be the cheering section. . . . Is Lola here?"

Lola, right. Lola's gone, turned into Medusa and slammed the door behind her. "She was," I say. "She got her forms and left." Without a word to me, or a glance in my direction; not even like she was snubbing me, but like I was invisible. Invisible to the infinite power.

Carma shrugs. "Maybe she'll be human again by Festival. Or as human as she ever gets."

"Maybe," Jef says, dubious.

I don't say anything.

"You have to see the auditorium there," Jef says to me. He and Carm are going there next year, to Crispin, they're both taking theater tech. "It's *huge*. And their dressing rooms, each dressing room is like as big as our whole scene shop—"

"Kit," says Carma around her CocoChunx, "would get lost there. He is a dupe for direction."

"He is not," Jef says. "I'd show him. . . . We'd have such a great time there, Kit, you know we would."

I smile. "I know."

Now "Sorry, sorry," Mick bustling from backstage, two steps at a time down to where we are, legs up on the seats and "Paperwork," he says, handing a floppy sheaf to me. A *Waiting for Beckett* T-shirt and new black jeans; he's shaping his stubble into a pointy little beard. "Have it all back to me by Monday. The travel stuff, and the permission forms—your parents sign here, and here—"

"Oh I can't wait." Carm stuffs candy wrappers in her pockets, shrugs into her coat. "We're going to win, I know it. We are going to win *so big*."

Mick smiles, head cocked back. "It's possible. It is definitely possible. Though I have to say, we'll be up against some real powerhouses—McCady Prep's going, and Don Frederick's kids from State—"

"Admissions people will be there," says Jef and raises his eyebrows at me.

They want me to go to Bib's with them, but I can't: I have to get going with all the college stuff, my essay, applications, I'm way behind.

At home I feed Pixy, then check my e-mail: another long one from Fran, nagging me to apply to Juilliard: *Take a chance, you owe it to yourself.* My mom thinks I should, too: *It's obvious you've got the gift, Kit. Like a butterfly from a cocoon. . . . Send an application, what can it hurt?* My dad says it's my decision, and I should do whatever I want most.

Pro bono? I say, joking.

That's right, he says. *All the way.*

They're treating me differently since the Blake thing, more like a, a grownup. A man. . . . Sometimes I catch my dad looking at me, with a face somewhere between his lawyer-face and his father-face. Wondering. Measuring. When I catch him, he laughs and *Just trying to figure you out,* he says.

What else have I gotten? A "hi!" from Alice Metsig, a silly joke from Jef, a sign-up thing from Camp Shakespeare, how did they get my name? My last e-mail to Lindsay is still in the outbox, I delete it. She'll never answer, she hates me now. The look on her face that night: *Big fucking joke.* Like the joke was on her, like I did it on purpose. Like I "did" anything! I just *was.* So why should I care, right? if she only wanted who she thought I was, not who I really am?

But I do care. Because she cared about me, only a little, but for real; I know she did. And now she'll never listen to me, never understand. . . . I don't feel sorry for her; Carm thinks I do, but I don't. I just wish it didn't hurt.

But no matter how she felt, about me, about everything, she's an actor. Opening night, she just went out there and blasted out to the back row, she called home *collect*. Her hair mussed and gleaming under the lights, make-up bruises like the real thing, she was Lola, she was Joan of Arc and Rosa Parks and every action-movie hero you ever saw; she was the one. Even though it wasn't what it could have, should have been, not what she—we—had done before: it wasn't deep anymore, just burn on the surface. But she burned, all right. They called us back six times for curtain calls. Her father was crying in the front row.

Afterwards I went up to her, I had to. There in the swirl of backstage chaos, everyone laughing and shouting and hugging, the TV guys hanging out by the door and I thought, no matter what, even if she spits in my face, I have to say it. So I planted myself right in front of her, where she couldn't not see me, and *Lindsay*, I said. *You are amazing. It was, it was an honor being onstage with you.*

She didn't say anything. Still made up, still in her prison costume, she just looked at me like she was a thousand miles away, a thousand miles straight up looking down. Then *Thanks*, she said, and walked away. And that was that.

She didn't go to the cast party, just talked to the TV guys and left with her dad. When the audience finally cleared out, Fran hauled out this giant trolley of stuff, soda and beer and chips, and a huge chocolate BREAK A LEG! cake. There were a million people there, parents, everybody, people who weren't even part of the show. Like Pablo. Wading through the crowd to me, arms out for a big bear hug: wrapped close and tight, my eyes closed, breathing in his scent and feeling, what? Sad? No. Not sad.

That fire scene, he said, stepping back. *Oh man, that was so cool! You were so cool!*

And Marc clapping me on the shoulder: *Kit, you were fantastic. Tell me you're going on to ADA. Or Juilliard—*

Maybe, I said. *I don't know yet.*

There was a lot I still didn't know, that night. . . . All that while, wanting Pablo, dodging Lindsay, and he was right there, right out in front of me. At rehearsal. In the car. At my side. With his little foresty dreads, his crooked smile. Wanting me. Jef-with-one-F.

Did you read my note?

After the cast party, he drove me home. In Carm's ice-cold car.

KIT + ME♥.

The streetlights through the window, flickering there-and-gone. His face: tense, sweet, hoping.

Didn't you know? Couldn't you tell? Every time I was around you, every time I even looked at you—

KIT + ME♥.

What had Carm said? *Somebody wrote it. Somebody who wants you.*

Wants me. And I was blind, or blindfolded, hands

pressed over my own eyes. . . . Carm knew, of course. Even though she didn't tell me, even though she tells me everything else in the damn world, but *He made me swear not to,* she said. And the memory: of her room, the printer's whir, hunting for her shoe: *There's no way Jef can tell you who wrote that.* Oh. I get it, now.

It's not like I imagined, all those poster-boy fantasies: hearts and flowers, waltzing away while the trumpet plays. We just go places, me and Jef, like Bib's, or the movies, and we eat popcorn, we drink chai and coffee, we talk, we laugh. Together. . . . It's not a dream, I guess, is the difference. It's real. Which means anything can happen, we could fall in love or not, there's no script. He's not Pretend Perfect Boyfriend, he's Jef, with his bandanna, and the little lightning-bolt scar on his arm, and his million knock-knock jokes. And his kiss.

And I'm—me. Like I was me onstage, taking Pablo and Blake and the window seat and everything I wanted and everything I was and just—pushing it out there. I made my own surface tension, that night, my own bubble world. Because I had to. And because I could. Because I'm an actor, too. The cocoon; the closet. Out onstage. I wanted to lose myself in a play, didn't I? become someone else? And then I turned into me, for real. Isn't that weird?

Whatever works, Carm says.

Red shirt, dark eyes, big Pablo grin. . . . I have other stuff tacked up there now, where that picture used to be: a poster from *Rent* that Mick gave me, the original production, and the program from *Talk* with my name inside: *Kit*

Webster as REED. A picture I tore out from *Cog,* of two guys on a hill, silhouetted in the sun, their arms around each other. And a photo of us, of me and Jef, that Carm took in Bib's parking lot: two guys smiling, in the sun, their arms around each other.

GOFISH

KATHE KOJA

What did you want to be when you grew up?
A writer, always.

When did you realize you wanted to be a writer?
When I first learned to read. I started writing stories when I was about five years old, as soon as I could use a pencil.

What's your first childhood memory?
Asking my father to read the comics to me on a Sunday morning.

What's your most embarrassing childhood memory?
Not going to tell you!

What's your favorite childhood memory?
Dancing with my teenage sister to the Beatles on TV. She had super-cool, white cat's-eye glasses, and she taught me how to twist and shout.

What was your worst subject in school?
Anything that really bored me (but mostly math, I'm sad to say).

What was your best subject in school?
Anything I really loved (but mostly English).

What was your first job?
Not counting babysitting? I was a server at a banquet hall the summer I was fifteen. Frat boys threw hunks of wet salad at me, and a drunk lady gave me a monster tip.

How did you celebrate publishing your first book?
I think I was too bowled over to celebrate! The thing I remember most is looking at the book again and again, so pleased that it was a real, physical object in the world.

Where do you write your books?
At my desk at home, on a Mac, surrounded by our cats. I admire people who can write in cafés, planes, hotel rooms, etc., but I just can't do it.

Where do you find inspiration for your writing?
There's nowhere it's not. And when I'm working on a specific novel or writing project, some inner antennae pop up, and, like a magpie, I notice details I can use for my story, hints and signposts, things everywhere. I think that's a kind of heightened awareness we all share: When you adopt a black puppy, say, suddenly you find the world is full of black puppies! Your inner eye has been opened to a particular subject, and you see it everywhere.

Which of your characters is most like you?
None are, and they all are. My novels aren't autobiographical, but I find shared characteristics in pretty much all the characters (even the mean ones).

When you finish a book, who reads it first?
While it's still being written, my friend and agent, Chris Schelling. When it's finished, my husband, Rick Lieder.

Are you a morning person or a night owl?
Morning. (Though it used to be night.)

What's your idea of the best meal ever?
Yummy vegetarian, something Thai or Indian: HOT.

Which do you like better: cats or dogs?
I love anything with four legs, but I'm at heart a cat person.

What do you value most in your friends?
A ferocious sense of humor and good taste in media.

Where do you go for peace and quiet?
Outside, into the grass and the trees. And sometimes to a church or zendo, for a different kind of quiet.

What makes you laugh out loud?
Absurdity.

What's your favorite song?
Impossible question. And whatever I picked, I'd think of something I liked even better in a minute. And by this time tomorrow, I might have a different answer altogether.

Who is your favorite fictional character?
This question is even more impossible! Just for starters, Harriet (the spy), Franny and Zooey, and Cormac McCarthy's Judge Holden. And any number of Flannery O'Connor's eccentrics. And White Fang and Buck, from Jack London's books. And . . .

What are you most afraid of?
Bad things happening to the ones I love.

What time of the year do you like best?
Spring and fall: the times of change.

What is your favorite TV show?
The Simpsons and *Deadwood.*

If you were stranded on a desert island, who would you want for company?
Someone who knew how to un-strand us!

If you could travel in time, where would you go?
Right now, I'm reading about the remarkable Russian poet Anna Akhmatova, so I'd love to go to the Stray Dog Café, in 1912 St. Petersburg, and meet her.

What's the best advice you have ever received about writing?
Don't wait for inspiration, just sit down and work, every day. Never wait until you "feel like" working.

What do you want readers to remember about your books?
The feeling of being another person for a time, of living and breathing someone else's experience. That's what I love best about reading, and what I hope to do for my readers, too.

What would you do if you ever stopped writing?
Be enormously unhappy.

What do you like best about yourself?
I don't give up easily. Also, I'm a pretty good dancer.

SQUARE FISH

What is your worst habit?
Impatience. Although I guess that's a character trait, not a habit. . . . Then let's say yelling at other drivers in traffic.

What is your best habit?
Empathy. Wait, that's another character trait!

What do you consider to be your greatest accomplishment?
I'm proud that I was able to raise my son (who's now twenty-two) and write my books and give my best to both at the same time.

Where in the world do you feel most at home?
At my desk, working.

What do you wish you could do better?
Physical, tactile things, like swimming, sewing, yoga.

What would your readers be most surprised to learn about you?
How shy I am.